EMILY LIME
LIBRARIAN
DETECTIVE

THE PENCIL CASE

www.davidficklingbooks.com

Also by Dave Shelton

Emily Lime
Librarian Detective:
The Book Case

Thirteen Chairs

A Boy and a Bear in a Boat

Good Dog, Bad Dog:
The Golden Bone

Good Dog, Bad Dog:
Double Identity

EMILY LIME
LIBRARIAN
DETECTIVE

THE PENCIL CASE

DAVE SHELTON

David Fickling Books

31 Beaumont Street
Oxford OX1 2NP, UK

Emily Lime – Librarian Detective: The Pencil Case
is a
DAVID FICKLING BOOK

First published in Great Britain by
David Fickling Books,
31 Beaumont Street,
Oxford, OX1 2NP

www.davidficklingbooks.com

Hardback edition published 2020
This edition published 2021

Text and illustrations © Dave Shelton, 2020

978-1-78845-104-8

1 3 5 7 9 10 8 6 4 2

Papers used by David Fickling Books are from well-
managed forests and other responsible sources.

MIX
Paper from
responsible sources
FSC® C018072

DAVID FICKLING BOOKS Reg. No. 8340307

A CIP catalogue record for this book is available from the British Library.

Typeset in 12/18pt Cambria by Falcon Oast Graphic Art Ltd.
Printed and bound in Great Britain by Clays Ltd, Elcograf S.p.A.

For all the librarians

ONE

Red-faced and breathless, Daphne Blakeway stepped through the door into the main hall of St Rita's School for Spirited Girls and surveyed the scene before her. Crisp winter-morning light angled in through the tall windows of the main hall onto the bustling pupils as they took their seats for the first morning assembly of the new term.

Something was up; Daphne felt it at once, though it took her a moment to recognize what it was. There was a buzz about the place, but it wasn't the usual near-riotous excitement that St Rita's girls conjured at the start of a day. This was something more constrained, more tense, like the air in an overinflated balloon waiting to explode. Not that explosions were so very unusual at St Rita's, of course, but usually they would be joyful occasions (except for Mrs Klinghoffer, the chemistry mistress) whereas now the mood in the hall seemed to be fearful.

Daphne scanned the rows of seated pupils for a particular face. As this particular face sat beneath an even more particular head of spectacularly unruly hair, and belonged to the only boy in the school, it was simple enough to locate it. She waved and smiled, and George gave a thin smile back as he lifted a book from the chair next to him.

'Where have you been?' he said, as Daphne shuffled along the row of fourth formers towards him. 'Are you going to be late at the start of *every* term?'

'Never mind that,' said Daphne, sitting. 'Why does it feel like someone's died? *Has* someone died?'

'Not this time.' George's tone implied that this would be preferable. 'The rumour is there's a new head coming in.'

'But why?' said Daphne. 'Miss Bagley was doing

such a good job as a stand-in. Some of the girls were even starting to *learn things*! Why not just give her the job permanently?'

'Search me.' George shrugged. 'Reckon her face just doesn't fit with the board of governors. So they've brought in this new woman called Woolley.'

He waved a finger in the direction of the stage where the St Rita's staff were assembled on a line of chairs, to the left of which Miss Bagley and another taller, formidable-looking woman stood in conversation.

A new voice, harsh and rasping, joined George and Daphne's conversation from the row behind them. 'Woolley, did you say? So the rumours are true, then? Well, well, well.'

George rolled his eyes. 'Hello, Cynthia.'

Daphne turned to face St Rita's head girl, Cynthia 'The Roar' Rawlinson, whose expression was even more smug and superior than usual.

'What's true?' asked Daphne.

'That our new head has come here from Wolfridge Manor.'

George's head snapped round. 'Wolfridge Manor?' he said in a cracked voice.

'That's right.' Cynthia gave a leering grin. 'My cousin there mentioned in her Christmas card that their deputy head, Miss Woolley, was leaving. And now it seems she's come here.'

'Oh, blimey!'

'Is, er . . . is that *bad*, then?' said Daphne.

'Well,' said George, 'Wolfridge has a reputation for, um, being a bit strict.'

'No it doesn't.' Cynthia's narrowed eyes glinted in the winter light. 'It has a reputation for being *extremely* strict. There'll be no more of Bagley's soft ways now she's here. We'll finally have what this place has always needed: some good firm discipline.' She crossed her arms and settled back in her chair. 'And I for one will be very glad to help her provide it.'

Daphne and George faced forward again.

'Of course it could be a *different* Miss Woolley,' said George, without a shred of conviction.

They watched the imposing figure towering over Miss Bagley, her face stonily serious.

'But if it's not?' said Daphne.

'If it's not,' whispered George, 'then that's very bad.'

Daphne nodded, then glanced to her side to see a familiar figure taking the seat next to her.

'What ho, Daffers!' said Marion Fink. 'Good Christmas?'

'Barely adequate,' said Daphne. 'But Auntie Millie gave me her old camera so that was nice at least. And you? I suppose you spent it in a castle or something, did you?'

'Oh no. Thank good-ness. Awfully draughty,

the castles, this time of year, and Pater simply *refuses* to heat them. No, I went to see Mummy, over in Monte Carlo.'

'Crikey! How was that?'

'Oh, it was fine, I suppose. But she'd given most of the staff time off over Christmas so I had to open all my presents for myself! Can you imagine?'

'Well . . .'

'It took *for ever*. And I still don't know how I'm supposed to get all those ponies shipped over here. I just don't think Mater really thought it through *at all*. Still, mustn't grumble, I suppose.'

Daphne thought back to the pair of barely identifiable socks that her granny had knitted her. 'No,' she said.

'Who are the new birds?' Marion twitched a finger in the direction of the staff seated on the stage.

'Well, apparently the new head is Miss Woolley – she's the one talking to Miss Bagley. And, let's see . . .'

Daphne took a closer look at the figures sitting across the stage. On the left, in the chairs closest to where the head and deputy were winding up their chat, were three new faces.

6

'They must be, um, physics, French and, erm . . .' Daphne checked across the row of teachers trying to work out who was missing from last term's line-up.

'Art,' said George. 'I assume that's the one with the frizzy hair and half a ton of jewellery.'

'Oh, lawks!' Marion wrinkled her nose in distaste. 'What a fright. And a shame too. I rather liked old Finnegan. She made a good fist of doing the scenery for the school play last term.'

'Yes,' said Daphne. 'She really put her heart into that.'

'Yes.' Marion frowned. 'Shame it all got destroyed in the dress rehearsal. But then giving Hemsby and Froome swords was never going to end well.'

'No,' said George, glancing up at the ceiling. 'And Mr Thanet still hasn't shifted that bloodstain.' His gaze fell back to the front where Miss Bagley was taking centre stage to address the hall. 'Ey up,' he said. 'Here comes the bad news.'

'Now then,' said Miss Bagley, with warm authority, 'let's have a bit of quiet, girls.' The low murmuring hum that had previously filled the room fell to near silence. 'As you know, or at least you should if you've been paying any attention at all, me being head last term was only ever meant to be temporary while the governors found . . . someone *proper* to fill the post permanently.' She paused, just for a moment, her face showing no sign of any emotion she might be feeling. 'So, as of right now, I am back to being your deputy head, and I'd like you all to welcome – with polite applause: Wilkins, thank you; you can put the catapult away and see me after – your new headmistress, Miss Woolley, who joins us from Wolfridge Manor.'

The mention of the new head's previous school set off a fresh buzz of alarm amongst the girls as Miss Woolley strode over to the spot that Miss Bagley had just vacated. George recognized Cynthia Rawlinson's distinctly gloating chuckle behind him.

'She does look a bit scary.' Daphne cast a worried look at Miss Woolley standing centre stage, strong and upright, staring out at her new charges. She raised a palm towards them and the room fell quiet. Miss Woolley paused, her face stern and unreadable, her lips pursed and utterly still.

Then, at last, she spoke, in a deep and booming voice that was just as intimidating as her stature.

'What an *opportunity*!' she said, scanning her audience with unnerving intensity.

Silence fell.

'As Miss Bagley said, I previously taught at Wolfridge Manor, which, I imagine some of you may know, has something of a reputation. The girls sent there are just like you. Very spirited. Some of them are . . . difficult, some rather troubled. All of them are *wild*.' She paused again. 'At least, they are when they arrive. But by the time they leave

they are polite. Orderly. Tamed.

'Obedience and conformity are the watchwords at Wolfridge. Obedience, conformity and, above all, *discipline*.' She drove a lumpen fist into the palm of the other hand to emphasize the word. 'Fierce . . . hard . . . *discipline*.' Three more emphatic thumps. 'These are the foundations of the successful running of a school that the headmistress at Wolfridge, Mrs Crowhurst, drummed into me. There can be no learning, she always told me, without discipline!' One last mighty thump sent a ripple of shock through the front few rows of girls.

Cynthia gave a squeak of pleasure.

Miss Woolley slowly turned her head first one way then the other, scanning the ranks of girls set out before her.

'So,' she said, 'as I'm sure you can all well imagine . . .' There was a glint in her eye, and her mouth tightened into an eager grin. But then her voice softened. 'I am *so relieved* to have finally got away from that *dreadful* place, and Mrs Crowhurst's positively medieval approach to education, and to have the chance, here at St Rita's, finally to use my own methods.' Miss Woolley raised her eyes to the ceiling and smiled. All the tension seemed to pass out of her body as if a great weight had been lifted from her. 'Because I am convinced, girls, that the real key to success lies not in obedience, but in freedom; not in conformity, but in self-expression; and not in discipline, but in *compassion*.'

The girls of St Rita's stared up at her in stunned silence.

'So, as of today, there will be no corporal punishment: no use of the cane; no rapping of knuckles with a ruler; no clips round the ear.'

Now it was the turn of several of the teachers seated behind Miss Woolley to look shocked.

'What about slippers, miss?' said a voice from the front row.

'I beg your pardon . . . I'm so sorry, young lady, I don't yet know your name.' Miss Woolley moved to the edge of the stage and leaned forward to address the girl who had spoken.

'Tilly, miss. Tilly Shaw.'

'Well, hello, Tilly Shaw. I'm very pleased to meet you. What's this about slippers?'

'Mrs Butler uses a slipper, miss. Instead of a cane or a ruler. She says it sounds better.'

'Oh, I see.' Miss Woolley glanced back over her shoulder at the muscular form of Mrs Butler, the music teacher. 'Well, Mrs Butler will be so kind as to give up her slipper. Staff will no longer strike pupils at all. I hope that is clear enough.'

By the look of disappointment on Mrs Butler's face it was all too clear.

'Yes, young lady?' Miss Woolley raised a finger and cast a twinkling smile toward the rear of the hall.

'What about the prefects?' Daphne and George looked round and recognized one of the more brutal sixth form girls, her hand raised and, out of habit, her fist clenched. 'You'll need someone to dish out thumpings if the teachers aren't doing it.'

'No!' Miss Woolley's voice was firm and defiant. 'No hitting of any kind. This is 1954, not the Dark Ages. There is no place in modern education for barbarism.'

'She's clearly never seen the lacrosse team in action,' whispered George.

'Or Matron,' said Daphne.

'In fact,' said Miss Woolley, 'we'll have no need for prefects.' The sixth form brute gave a disappointed whine. 'You girls must be shown that you are all equal, for how else can you thrive and blossom? So: no prefects; no head girl.'

There was a strangled yelp from Cynthia.

'No punishments,' continued the head. 'We' – she spread her arms wide to indicate the despondent and horrified array of staff behind her – 'offer you the gift of knowledge. Of enrichment. Of enlightenment. And you must all be free to embrace this opportunity in your own way.' She raised her arms higher and beamed out at her audience. 'Then we can all advance together into an exciting new future – confident, hopeful and free from fear.'

Daphne and George, and pretty much everyone else, gawped at her in amazement.

'And to help me deliver you into that bright future, you will have seen that there are some other new faces here alongside me.'

Miss Woolley gestured to the three women on

the furthest left chairs.

'Mrs Fotheringay joins us from St Randolph's and replaces Miss Merrick as physics mistress . . .'

A wide-eyed young woman rose briefly from the end seat, wearing the expression of a small but delicious mammal surrounded by ravenous wolves.

'Miss Deakins has come with me from Wolfridge Manor and replaces Miss Finnegan in the art room.'

Confirming George's earlier guess, the flamboyantly dressed and bejewelled woman with

wild curly hair stood confidently from her chair and beamed out at the children.

'And indeed Miss Deakins will soon be leading an outing to the Pilkington Art Gallery, as the first of a programme of trips out of the school to expand the bounds of your education. Sign-up sheets will be posted shortly, just as soon as we've booked transportation. Unfortunately all the local coach hire firms seem to be unusually busy at the moment.'

Miss Woolley was alone in looking puzzled about this.

'And Miss Quirk will take over from Mrs Hayes as your French mistress.'

The third teacher, in severe clothes and with a severe haircut, rose to cast a severe stare around the hall.

'Well, she looks jolly, I don't think,' whispered Marion.

'I'm sure you'll do your best to give us all a warm welcome. We're so excited to be here, and looking forward to a long and fruitful time together.' Miss Woolley beamed out at the girls of St Rita's, her face a shining portrait of courageous hope.

'I give her a week,' said George.

TWO

'Aren't you worried, though?' said Daphne as she and George picked their way between bustling girls, heading towards the library.

'What about?' George lazily ducked his head to avoid a viciously hurled rubber.

'Miss Woolley, of course! She might not be the terror that you expected, but—'

'Oh, I wouldn't worry about her.' George swerved round a pair of scrapping second formers. 'She might cause a bit of a to-do in the rest of the school for a while, but we'll be all right in the library.'

'I hope you're right,' said Daphne, ducking herself as the rubber came pinging back at twice the speed of before and connected with the back of Cynthia Rawlinson's head.

Cynthia spun round, fury brimming in her as she instantly identified the guilty thrower. 'Hessett!' she yelled, clenched all over but most especially at the end of her sleeves.

The third former in question flinched out of habit, then drew herself up to her full height of not very much and stared back defiantly.

'What are you going to do, Cynthia? You're not head girl any more, remember?'

Cynthia's face froze and she seemed to visibly

shrink as George and Daphne passed her.

'She's not a Roar,' said Hessett behind them. 'More like a squeak now.'

'I really hope you're right,' said Daphne.

'After you,' said George as he and Daphne arrived at the bottom of the steps leading up to the library door.

Daphne's hand trembled a little as she placed it on the handrail and went up.

'Blimey, Daffers, are you nervous?'

Daphne gave a small laugh. 'More like excited,' she said, pausing outside the door. 'I was just remembering going in on my first day. All those empty bookcases!'

'Crammed to bursting now,' said George. 'Me and Lime finished shelving a couple of days back.'

'It must look amazing,' said Daphne, her hand on the door handle but still not turning it.

'But . . . ?' said George.

'But I'm also remembering my first meeting with Emily Lime. And . . .' she gulped, 'the Beast.'

The Beast was the library cat, a terrifying and vicious animal that often left 'gifts' of dead animals and sometimes had to be fended off with a chair.

'Actually,' said George, 'we haven't seen the Beast at all lately. Not since before Christmas. So you're all right on that score.'

'It just disappeared?'

'Yuss. It does that sometimes. But don't worry, it always comes back.' George gave his chin a thoughtful rub. 'Or do I mean *do* worry, it always comes back? Either way, it's not in residence at the moment.'

'And Emily Lime?'

'Ah, well, *that* loathsome creature is very much still here, I'm afraid. But you can't have everything. Now get in, will you?' George nodded at the door.

Daphne pushed it open with a loud creak. 'Mr Thanet still hasn't oiled the hinges then?' she said, stepping inside. 'As caretakers go, he really is— Oh!'

The door of the library let into a small raised area from which steps led down into the library proper. It was an odd arrangement that seemed to have no good architectural reason behind it, but it gave a fine view of the whole library. Daphne stood in silence for a moment, taking it in.

'Oh!' she said. 'It's beautiful!'

And it was.

All the previously empty shelves were now filled with pristine books, their pages crisp, uncreased, unmarked and perfect, standing straight and proud like soldiers. Shafts of winter light angled in through the tall windows lending the scene an extra magnificence.

'It's like a cathedral of books!'

George gave a thoughtful nod. 'Not too shabby, is it?'

There was a clattering of sensible shoes briskly crossing bare wooden boards, and a short girl in wonky glasses and a red beret appeared from behind one of the bookcases and frowned up at Daphne and George.

'Oh. You're here,' she said. 'Well, come on, then. We haven't got all day.'

'Nice to see you too, Emily Lime,' said Daphne as she headed down the steps. 'Happy New Year,' she muttered to herself. 'And how was your Christmas?

Oh, how kind of you to ask. My Christmas was very nearly adequate, thank you. And how—'

'Stop that mumbling,' said Emily Lime. 'Don't you know this is a library?'

'Yes,' said Daphne, still taking in her surroundings and running a finger along some of the books. 'And it seems to be a brilliant one. Well done, Emily Lime.' She gave a nod of approval.

Emily Lime's mouth twitched in an uncomfortable manner which, after a little thought, Daphne realized must have been some kind of a smile.

Daphne took a few moments to tour the full extent of the room, observing as she went the study tables with chairs arranged around them at perfectly regular intervals, the immaculate issuing desk, the general neatness, tidiness and spick and spanness of the whole place.

'What is it that we haven't got all day for?' she said as she arrived back beside the others. 'It looks like you've already done everything.'

Emily Lime frowned and twitched and paced, shooting glances to all corners as if trying to catch some tiny imperfection by surprise. 'We haven't done *everything*, though, have we?' she barked. 'We haven't—'

The door creaked open. George turned to look, but Daphne kept her attention on Emily Lime.

'We haven't what?' said Daphne.

'We haven't opened yet,' said Emily Lime, and for once her voice was small and quiet.

Daphne stared at her, and she thought that maybe, just possibly, Emily Lime looked frightened as she too turned her head towards the door.

'. . . and this is our library,' said Miss Bagley,

ushering in Miss Woolley and the three new teachers. 'And these are the herberts who run it.' Miss Bagley threw a warm smile at the three children as she descended with the others into the main area of the library. 'At least, they're in charge until Mrs Crump, the librarian, returns from sick leave,' she said. 'And they've not done badly so far, I hope you'll agree.'

'Oh, indeed!' Miss Woolley nodded her approval as she surveyed the towering shelves. 'An excellent job.' She turned her attention to the children and smiled. 'And did you really build it back up from nothing?'

'Yes, miss,' said Daphne. 'Actually, we helped solve a case for the police, and the reward money paid for all the books.'

'Really?' said Miss Quirk, looking as if she might sprain an eyebrow in her expression of disbelief.

'Actually, yes,' said Miss Bagley. 'A bank robbery.'

'Good gracious,' said Miss Woolley, giving each of them in turn a rather closer look now.

'How thrilling!' said Miss Deakins, her jewellery jangling as she threw her hands to her face in excitement. 'You must tell me *all* about it. You should all sign up for the art gallery trip and tell me all about it on the way there.'

'That's very kind of you,' said George, 'only we'll need to stay here and look after things.'

'Yes,' said Daphne. 'Now we're ready to open again, this is when the proper library work begins: issuing library tickets, stamping the books, reshelving . . .'

'Breaking up fights, first aid . . .' said George.

'Oh no, no, no.' Miss Woolley shook her head.

'I'm afraid so, miss,' said George. 'We have to be realistic. There are bound to be injuries.'

'Oh no, I didn't mean the fighting. A little enthusiastic competition in pursuit of learning is rather a healthy sign, I'd say. But library tickets? I'm not sure I really see the need.'

There was a long pause during which three young jaws fell so far and so hard that they temporarily ceased to work at all.

'Excuse me?' said Daphne, recovering first.

'I don't see the need for library cards. They'd only make extra work for you all, and you've clearly done enough already.'

'Eh?' said George.

'So rather than all that fiddly business with cards, and rubber stamps, and dates and suchlike, why don't we just let the girls take whatever books they want, and then bring them back once they've finished with them?'

'What?!' said Emily Lime.

'That way it's so much more welcoming,' said Miss Woolley. 'And you three can have a well-deserved rest.' She tapped her chin with a contemplative finger, her face darkened by thought as she weighed up what she'd just said. 'Yes. No need for library cards.' She gave a decisive nod. 'And come to think of it' – she raised her eyebrows, as if struck by a revelation – 'no need for librarians.'

There was an awkward silence that held within it all manner of possibilities. Then Emily Lime broke that silence with an unearthly scream and had to be physically restrained by Daphne and George.

'NO NEED FOR LIBRARIANS?! *NO NEED?*'

'Maybe we should show Miss Deakins the art room now,' said Miss Bagley.

'By all means,' said Miss Woolley, turning to follow Miss Bagley out. She glanced over at Emily Lime snarling and clawing at the air as Daphne and George struggled to hold her back. 'You see,' the new head said, 'this is just the sort of passionate free expression that was so lacking at Wolfridge Manor. This really is most encouraging.'

The other teachers followed her out, each glancing back, Mrs Fotheringay alarmed, Miss Deakins sympathetic, and Miss Quirk appalled.

'SHE'S A MANIAC!' screeched Emily Lime, as the door swung closed behind them.

'It does seem . . . a bit rash,' said Daphne.

'No library cards? It'll be anarchy!' Emily Lime clutched at her head, scrunching her beret alarmingly. 'And a library is no place for anarchy. The whole place will be stripped bare in under a week.'

'And probably on fire,' said George. 'Again.'

Emily Lime considered this, her face hardening. 'Well, that settles it,' she said. 'She'll have to go.'

'Oh, well that's a bit drastic,' said Daphne. 'I really thought that a lot of the girls were calming down last term. Maybe it won't be so bad.'

THREE

I t *was* so bad.

It was oh so bad.

It had been quite bad when they first opened the library on Tuesday. Now it was Thursday and it was very bad indeed.

'This is very bad,' said Daphne, raising her voice to be heard over the noise.

George, crouching beside her behind the issuing desk, gave her a withering look. He meant to try a withering comment too, but he was distracted by the book that hit his head.

'Ow!' he said instead.

Emily Lime, crawling on all fours, retrieved the book from the floor, dusted it off, and checked it for damage. 'Hmf . . . no great harm done,' she said, casting a narrow resentful look over the top of the desk.

'Well, maybe not to the bloomin' book, but what about my poor head?'

Emily Lime inspected George's head for much less time than she'd spent on the book. 'Slightly scuffed but in generally sound condition,' she said. 'Externally, at least. And anyway, your head will mend itself. My beautiful books won't.' She scowled. 'And it's all that idiot woman's fault!' She handed the book to Daphne.

'*A History of Trench Warfare*,' Daphne read from the spine. 'How apt.' She raised herself up to peek over the top of the desk and take stock of the madness beyond. 'Well,' she said to George, 'I suppose on the bright side at least it's busy. It would have been awful if we'd opened and nobody had come.'

George raised his slightly scuffed head above the parapet too, and winced at the view that greeted him. 'I hardly think,' he said, 'that it would have been worse than this.' He nodded towards the mayhem before them, then ducked to one side as another book whistled past his ear and was deftly caught by Emily Lime.

It was chaos.

But it wasn't just chaos. After all, this was St Rita's School for Spirited Girls: chaos was normal. This was different. This was chaos *in the library*. And that seemed like a whole new level of wrong. It looked to George a lot like war, albeit a war between armies wearing identical uniforms of pinafores and stockings. Of course, at St Rita's, fighting was a daily event. But previously he'd watched it from a safe distance. And he didn't like it even then. At close quarters, and in the confined space of the library, it was terrifying. *And* they were throwing books at each other! Books!

George couldn't bear to watch any longer; he ducked down behind the desk and turned round to sit with his back against it, feeling it shudder each time some new skirmish ran into it.

He clutched his knees to his chest. There was a quiet *tink*, barely audible amidst the roar of the battle, as something small bounced off the top of the desk and flew over George's head.

'Was that a *tooth*?' he said, already knowing the answer.

Emily Lime scrabbled on the floor for it and held it up for a closer look. 'Bicuspid,' she said. 'And badly neglected too. No wonder it came out. Whoever it belongs to is a very neglectful brusher.'

'Oh no!' said George, hearing the creak of the door even above the racket of combat. 'Who's this now?'

Daphne took a peek. 'It's Erica,' she said. 'And she's heading our way.'

The small rat-faced girl in question ducked and weaved through the mêlée with admirable skill and arrived at the desk unscathed.

'Oi!' she said, with characteristic charm. 'Post for

you. Bagley sent me over with it. Didn't realize it'd be a war zone, though. You should pay me danger money.'

'You'll be lucky,' said George, rising far enough to take a look at the pile of post she was carrying. 'Oh! Have we got a parcel?'

Erica scowled at him. 'No,' she said. 'That's mine. From me gran.' She plucked a handful of envelopes from the top of the pile and slapped them down into George's palm. 'These are yours.'

'Oh,' said George. 'Oh well. Ta.'

He sat back down as Erica scuttled away.

'Anything good?' said Daphne.

'One for you, the rest look like bills.'

He handed the single handwritten envelope to Daphne, then tore open the first of the others, extracted the paperwork from inside, and groaned.

'Oh, it's a letter from Veronica,' said Daphne, examining her own post, as George groaned again, more loudly this time, at the bill inside his second envelope.

'It sounds like her new school in Devon is . . . a bit of a change from here,' Daphne went on.

'Lucky her,' said George. 'Not inhabited by lunatics and run by a madwoman, then?'

'Well, no,' said Daphne. 'But she says she misses us all. That's nice.'

'Lovely,' growled George. 'Now, Lime, what did I tell you about keeping to a strict budget?'

'I have no idea,' said Emily Lime as she caught another flying book and added it to a growing pile on the floor beside her. 'Was it important?'

George made a strangled sort of noise. 'Yes, of *course* it was important. That's why I said at the time *now listen carefully, this is really important!* Don't you remember?'

'No,' said Emily Lime. 'I didn't think it was import-ant.' She shot a hand up and plucked another book from the air, preventing it from smashing through the window.

'Why? Why would you think it wasn't important?'

Emily Lime added the book to her neat stack. 'Because *you* said it.'

George rose up in what he hoped was an impos-ing manner and waved the bills in Emily Lime's face. 'You are bloomin' *impossible*, Lime!' he said. 'You've already spent more than all of the money! How are we meant to—'

Then a copy of *Ballistics for Beginners* hit him hard on the back of the head, and he decided that he should have a little lie-down.

Admiring the floorboards for a moment while he waited for the ringing sound in his ears to go away, George glanced first at Daphne, and then at Emily Lime. Neither of them, he concluded, looked delighted by the current situation, but even so he was able to spot a subtle change in their expressions as they stared out over the desktop: Daphne's lips parted and her eyebrows climbed further up her

34

forehead; Emily Lime's sour scowl tightened.

'Oh no!' said Daphne. 'That's all we need!'

George scrabbled up to see what they were seeing. Even glimpsed through a distracting mass of flailing limbs, flying fists and occasional spurts of blood, the imposing figure of the new arrival was unmistakeable.

'Hulky!' said George. 'Oh, blimey!'

Seraphina 'Hulky' Holcroft was, indeed, powering straight towards the issuing desk, with any girls in her way either fleeing, bouncing off her, or getting trampled underfoot. George studied her face

as she advanced towards them, trying to read her expression. It wasn't easy, but George eventually concluded that either she was concentrating very hard or she was furiously angry. A scrapping pair of third formers pirouetted into her path and crashed into her. Hulky swept them aside with one arm without breaking her stride. Two lumpen fists crashed down onto the desk as she leaned on it, looming over the cowering figures of George and Daphne.

Then Emily Lime stepped forward between them. 'How can we help?' she said.

Hulky raised her gaze to Emily Lime and pondered the question. It was a slow and painful process. 'I'm looking . . . for a book,' she said at last.

Emily Lime nodded. 'Very good,' she said. 'Anything in particular?'

'Miss . . . Deakins sent me,' she said.

'The new art mistress?' said Daphne, as she and George rose from the floor.

'Yurss.'

George, Daphne and Emily Lime stood there, safe in the shelter of Hulky's massive frame, as the blizzard of flying books and general pandemonium continued behind her.

'She sent me for a book,' said Hulky.

George and Daphne nodded attentively.

'About an artist,' said Hulky.

'Righto,' said George. 'And, er . . . does this artist have a name?'

'Well, obviously!' Hulky glowered at George. 'I'm trying to remember it.' She set about thinking again. They watched the painful contortions of her face and waited, more or less patiently, for further details to emerge.

'Paul . . . something or other . . . um . . .'

'Cezanne?' said Daphne.

Hulky shook her head.

'Nash?' said George.

'No!' said Hulky.

Then Emily Lime said something that was lost amid the shrieking of a passing pair of keen amateur wrestlers from the lower sixth.

Hulky's expression heaped annoyance on top of all the other boiling emotions it already contained. She turned and grabbed hold of the offending shriekers.

'WILL YOU ALL . . .' she bellowed.

'. . . JUST . . .' She raised the now silent and

terrified sixth formers into the air.

'. . . PLEASE . . .' She threw one girl sprawling across a nearby table.

'. . . BE . . .' She threw the other girl off towards the biography section where she landed on the hockey team captain, Miriam Wagstaffe.

'. . . quiet?'

By this point, they already were. Quiet, and still, and gaping, and afraid. But to make sure of her point, Hulky raised a finger to her lips.

'Shh,' she said very quietly. 'This *is* a library, you know.' Then she turned back to face Emily Lime. 'Pardon me?'

'Klee,' said Emily Lime.

A bright new dawn broke across Seraphina 'Hulky' Holcroft's face. 'Yes, that's it!'

Emily Lime showed no emotion and merely gave a small nod. 'Paul Klee,

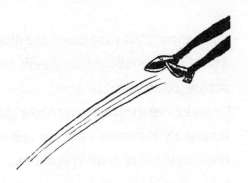

Swiss painter, 1879–1940.'

Hulky nodded vigorously, still grinning, while behind her every other girl in the library (except for Miriam Wagstaffe, who was unconscious) tiptoed meekly towards the exit.

'We have a very good book on him,' said Emily Lime, stepping out from the desk.

'Dewey number 759.9,' said George.

'This way,' said Daphne, and the four of them set off, picking their way across the book-strewn floor towards the art section as the door creaked closed behind the last of the other girls leaving, and a beautiful calm descended.

The Ks, it turned out, had been mercifully untouched by the recent unpleasantness, and the book about Paul Klee was easily located. There was a brief dispute about who should have the honour of retrieving it from the shelf, but in the end, neither George, nor Daphne nor Emily Lime could reach it, and by the time they fetched the library steps Hulky had taken it down for herself and was leafing through it contentedly at one of the study tables. They were less able to help with her other request for books on Abstract Expressionists (or *Object Impressionists* as Hulky misremembered it), but Emily Lime found a chapter in a book called *Modern Movements* and handed that over at least.

'So, do I need a . . . ticket or something, then?' Hulky scratched her head.

Daphne and George looked to Emily Lime, whose face twitched and flinched for some time before she

replied.

'No,' she said eventually, her voice strangled. 'Just... take them. And bring them back when you've finished with them.'

Hulky looked puzzled. 'Really?' she said.

'Yes,' squawked Emily Lime. 'Orders of the head. No tickets.'

Hulky stood, picked up her books, mumbled her thanks and Emily Lime saw her out.

'Of course, according to the orders of the head,' said Daphne, 'we shouldn't even be here. No librarians.'

'Ah, well,' said George, 'the Lime has an answer to that: Miss Woolley said there should be no *librarians*, but of course Lime is an *assistant* librarian, and we're *assistant assistant* librarians, so Woolley can't complain.'

'I'm not sure she'd see it that way,' said Daphne.

'I don't see why not,' said Emily Lime as she arrived back. 'I thought she was trying to encourage creative thinking. Now, you two start clearing up this mess. I need to order some books about Abstract Expressionism.'

'No you bloomin' don't,' George growled, though

he had already obediently started picking up books from the floor. '*If* there's any money left at all then we probably ought to spend it on a bucketload of glue.' He held up a mathematics text book that was close to falling apart.

'Oh, for heaven's sake!' said Emily Lime. 'We'll get some money. Something will turn up. It always does.'

'Oh yes?' said George. 'How, exactly? Are you going to solve another bank robbery and get another reward?'

'Oh, don't be so petty!' Emily Lime gave him a belligerent frown. 'This is a library – it has to have books.'

'Yes,' said George. 'But it can't have *all the books*, which seems to be your plan.'

He'd meant it as a joke, but Emily Lime looked as if she was giving it some serious thought. First there was a wide-eyed look of wonder, as Emily Lime imagined (George presumed) the endless shelves of her dream library, with every book in its right place. Then she looked about her at the not-so-dreamlike state of her real-world library and her face fell.

'At least things should be a little bit quieter

tomorrow,' said Daphne.

George and Emily Lime looked at her blankly.

'It's the trip to the art gallery,' said Daphne. 'So that will be a busload fewer girls here to make trouble.'

'Imagine. A busload of St Rita's girls let loose in a haven of culture and gentle contemplation of the arts!' said George. 'It's utter madness.'

Daphne nodded.

'Of course,' said George, 'we have to go.'

FOUR

'Why do we have to go?' said Emily Lime the next day, as George pushed her out of the back door of the school and into the bracing morning air. 'It's obviously going to be a disaster.'

'Of course it is, Lime. That's the point.' George kept Emily Lime moving with a series of gentle nudges. 'Taking St Rita's girls on an outing to Pilkington Art Gallery? It'll even make Sports Day look civilized.'

'And *when* it's a disaster,' said Daphne, bringing up the rear, 'we'll be there to take photographs as evidence.' She briefly lifted the box Brownie camera that was strung round her neck. 'Oh, hello, Miss C. Aren't you coming with us?'

Miss Cosgrove the Latin mistress, kneeling beside her motorbike, turned her oil-smeared face towards them as they passed. 'Oh yes!' she grinned. 'But have you seen that rust bucket of a bus? *And* they've got Mr Thanet driving it. So I'm going to make my own way there.' She patted her motorcycle fondly. 'Just treating Betty here to a bit of a tune-up before we set off. Got a spare helmet if any of you want a lift.'

'Um, no, ta very much,' said George. 'We'll take our chances on the bus.'

'Suit yourselves,' said Miss Cosgrove, cheerily waving a spanner at them, and returning her attention to her carburettor.

'Mr T is driving the bus?' said Daphne. 'This bus?' She pointed at the sorry-looking vehicle parked outside the school's front door.

'Yuss,' said George. 'It was the only one the hire company was willing to let us have. And they wouldn't supply a driver at all.'

'But Thanet can hardly control his bicycle,' squawked Emily Lime, 'let alone that death trap!'

'I'm sure he'll be fine,' said George, pushing Emily Lime up into the bus and trying to ignore the creaking sounds that resulted. 'Now stop complaining. You're lucky I managed to wangle us places on the trip at all. I owe, mmm . . . Miss Bagley, no end of favours for this.' George gave a friendly nod to Mr Thanet as they passed him sitting nervously in

46

the driver's seat, but he didn't look up. 'And even then we only got in because some fourth formers got sick and had to drop out.'

'Oh yes,' said Daphne. 'Erica and her friends gorged themselves on a whole box of chocolates that her gran sent her yesterday. Now they're all in the san with upset tummies.'

'That'll teach 'em not to share.' George herded Emily Lime into a seat halfway along the bus, then wedged himself in beside her so she couldn't escape.

'Still, it's a good thing for us they didn't.' Daphne sat across the aisle. 'Now we get to witness exactly how disastrous this trip will be, and we'll have photographic evidence of Miss Woolley's failings as a head that we can show to the board of governors.'

'Or the Board of Education,' said George.

'Or the police,' said Daphne.

'Whoever can get rid of the daft trout the fastest.'

Emily Lime considered this. 'I hope you have plenty of film,' she said, and pulled a book from her satchel and began to read.

George looked away from her and watched the other girls getting onto the bus.

'Move yourselves, you little squirts!' a sixth

former commanded some smaller girls. 'Sit down! And no trouble on the way there, or you'll have me to answer to!'

The older girl distributed her flock efficiently into seats, then sat herself at the back. Meanwhile another sixth former had come aboard with more younger girls whom she likewise seated with gruff efficiency before joining her friend on the back seat.

'Odd,' George said to Daphne. 'Why are the Sixes suddenly so keen on good behaviour?'

'What ho, Georgie!' George turned to see a familiar figure standing next to him.

'Oh, hello, Marion. I didn't know you were coming along.'

'No. Well, I wouldn't usually bother.' Marion lowered her voice to what she wrongly imagined was a whisper. 'Can't bear galleries and museums and whatnot. Who wants to spend hours in a draughty old building full of ancient relics? I get enough of that at home.'

A gaggle of fifth formers tutted at Marion as they tried to push past her.

Marion continued regardless. 'But Daddy wanted me to check on the Rembrandt he loaned them, the old fusspot, so I said I would.'

'Out of the way, Fink.' Another sixth former threw Marion a stare like a house brick.

Marion didn't notice. 'I don't know why he cares, to be honest. It's not even one of the good ones.'

'Come on, Marion,' said the girl ahead of Marion in the aisle, in a faint, fluting voice. She was tallish and broadish, with a slightly ruddy complexion, more or less like Marion herself, in fact, but with the volume turned down. 'You're holding everyone up.'

'Eh? Oh, righto, Cicely. Can't have that, can we?' She smiled at George and bustled off.

The remaining girls quickly found seats and settled down, Miss Quirk and Mrs Fotheringay counted everyone on board several times over, then Mr Thanet set the ancient bus noisily into motion, and Miss Deakins stood beside him and addressed the girls.

'Now, my lovelies,' she said, 'can I just say how it makes my heart positively *soar* to see you all so excited about our little outing today. I'm afraid that art was not something that the head of Wolfridge Manor had very much time for. I tried in vain to persuade her of the great power that culture has to enrich the minds of the young. So, truly, I am thrilled to find you so much more receptive to it.' She made an expansive gesture to express just how thrilled she was, but this was cut short when the bus swerved suddenly as Miss Cosgrove overtook it on her motorbike and Mr Thanet jerked the steering wheel as he flinched at the sudden noise. Miss Deakins stumbled sideways and had to cling to the back of Mr Thanet's seat for support.

'Sorry,' said Mr Thanet.

Miss Deakins threw him a dark look as she regained her balance. 'I must ask, though,' she went on, 'that you try to contain that excitement, and be on your best behaviour, both in the gallery and on the journey there.'

George leaned across the aisle towards Daphne. 'She'll be lucky,' he whispered.

Miss Deakins continued, her voice swooping as Mr Thanet swung the bus onto the road. 'Mr Thanet, who has so kindly agreed to drive us today, tells me that this bus is – what was the phrase he used . . . ?'

'An accident waiting to happen,' said Mr Thanet, loudly and clearly enough that the whole bus could hear him.

'Ah, yes,' said Miss Deakins. 'How apt. So if you could please refrain from any acts likely to cause any more bits to fall off it, then that would greatly increase our chances of arriving safely. Similarly, do please try *not* to distract Mr Thanet' – she wagged a finger at the girl seated in front of George who had been preparing to launch a manky-looking apple at Thanet's back – 'so that he can give his full attention to nursing this delicate vehicle to its destination.'

The girl stayed her hand and the apple remained unchucked, though whether this was as in response to Miss Deakins' advice or to the threatening glare of the sixth form girl seated across the aisle, George couldn't tell.

'All these sixth formers seem very keen for every-one to behave,' said Daphne.

'I think,' said George, 'they're just making sure we get there safely.'

'Out of a sense of responsibility?' Daphne sounded dubious. 'Or a love of art?'

'A love of betting on horse races, more like,' said Emily Lime. 'Racing at Pilkington starts at two p.m.'

They arrived at the gallery very nearly on time. The more or less good behaviour of the passengers continued throughout the journey due to the vigilance of the sixth formers over the younger girls, and Mr Thanet barely got lost at all. Miss Deakins had to direct him through the town to the museum where Miss Cosgrove, loitering on the pavement and smoking a cigarette, looked as if she was tired of waiting for them.

'Now, girls . . .' Miss Deakins stood and addressed them again, raising her voice above the grinding of gears as Mr Thanet tried to park. 'I know you will all be eager to see every last picture in the gallery, but I would advise restraint. Do not gorge yourself on *all* of the art or you will appreciate none of it.' The bus juddered to a halt as Mr Thanet abandoned his first attempt. Miss Deakins juddered to a halt for a moment too.

'Bloomin' 'eck, Mr T,' called out a second former. 'You made a right pig's ear of that!'

Mr Thanet shot her a dark look and ground the gear lever into reverse. The bus lurched backwards and promptly stalled.

'Gawd's sake, you useless pudding!'

'Now, now,' said Miss Deakins, though her expression suggested that she agreed with the girl's assessment of Mr Thanet's driving skills. 'As I was saying: don't try to see too much. Better to select a few particularly delicious works and really take the time to savour them. And you should all spend some time in the temporary exhibition of abstract art. *So* thrilling to see such a fresh approach!'

'Oi, Thanet!' shouted someone. 'Better take a fresh approach to parking this junkheap too if you don't want to flatten that lamppost.'

Mr Thanet stamped on the brakes, sending Miss Deakins staggering backwards.

'Here, let me do it, or we'll be 'ere all bloomin' day!' The second former stamped down the aisle and indicated with a jerk of the thumb that Mr Thanet should vacate the driver's seat. Mr Thanet glanced up at Miss Deakins, who gave a shrug.

'Go on then, Lydia,' sighed Thanet, standing.

The second former jumped into his place, sitting awkwardly on the edge of the seat so that her feet could reach the pedals, and revved the engine.

'Careful. The clutch is a bit tricky, and—'

Lydia dropped the clutch, arced the bus into the parking spot at frightening speed, reversed to straighten up, and yanked on the handbrake. Then she turned off the engine and dropped down from the driver's seat.

'Right then,' she said, smiling up at Miss Deakins. 'Let's go devour some of this 'ere culture then, shall we?'

FIVE

'**O**h my!'

Alfred, the gallery attendant, rose from his chair at the sight of a girl in St Rita's uniform entering the Greek room. Sally Cummings was in the first form, and slightly built, and Alfred steeled himself to demand that she leave at once. Previous visits by St Rita's girls had variously resulted in breakages, injury, trauma and a statue of the goddess Athena having its arms removed and then reattached using chewing gum. As such, they were not welcome.

But then Alfred spotted the two burly sixth form girls just behind Sally, each of them three times her size in all directions. He paused, awkwardly half-risen from his chair, and reconsidered. Perhaps it was unfair to assume that *all* St Rita's girls could not be trusted. As a further uniformed mob entered, Alfred concluded that they should indeed be allowed the benefit of the doubt. He gently lowered himself back onto his chair and pretended to contemplate a nearby Hercules.

'There's a bloomin' army of them!' he muttered to himself, and felt his heart flutter in a way that it hadn't done since his army days. Sparing a thought for his doctor, who had advised Alfred to avoid stressful situations, he resolved to let them pass unchallenged. After all, there were six members of school staff present to keep them in hand. And

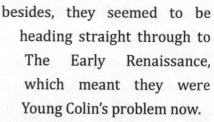

besides, they seemed to be heading straight through to The Early Renaissance, which meant they were Young Colin's problem now.

Miss Deakins brought them all to a halt in the

middle of the room, then Miss Woolley addressed them.

'Oh, my dears, what a treat to bring you all here, and to share in this adventure with you all. What a wealth of art, of history, of transcendent human endeavour you have here to experience. What a treasure trove! Now, you are all, of course, entirely free to spend your time as you wish. Neither I nor Miss Deakins would want in any way to influence your choices. You learn best when you teach your-selves. So go! Explore! Discover!'

The head waved her arms out wide, in a grand gesture that almost hit Miss Deakins in the face. Mr Thanet leaned in and whispered in Miss Woolley's ear.

'Oh, yes,' she said, her arms slowly lowering. 'Meet back here at four o'clock ready to take the bus back to school. Right, that's all, off you go.'

There were four doors leading out of the Early Renaissance room. Miss Woolley and Mrs Fotheringay strode happily off through the one to the left. Miss Deakins and Mr Thanet wandered off, chatting together, towards the one on the right. Miss Cosgrove went straight on and Miss Quirk stayed put.

'What do you think, then, Daffers?' said George. 'Shall we take a look at some of this here art while we wait for things to warm up? Then once the girls are doing their stuff and calamity abounds we can visit the hot spots, you can catch the worst of it on film, and with a bit of luck we'll have Woolley sacked before you know it.'

'Er, yes.' Daphne looked up from examining her camera as a group of sixth formers headed past and back the way they had come in. 'That's odd. I wouldn't have thought that the Sixes would be interested in classical sculpture.'

George glanced round after them and laughed. 'Don't be daft. They're not interested in the Greek statues. They're heading for the exit and off to the racecourse, I reckon. Deakins won't be pleased. This trip is s'posed to be mostly for their benefit

58

and most of 'em have left without pointing a single eyeball at any art.'

'Jolly good,' said Daphne, raising her camera to her eye and pressing the shutter. 'Truancy.'

'Pff,' said George. 'We'll have richer pickings than that soon enough, I bet. Where shall we start?'

'Let's try the Nineteenth Century room,' said Daphne.

'Good idea,' said Emily Lime, from behind the book she was reading. 'They have the best chairs there.'

'Bloomin' 'eck, Lime, you might take your head out of a book for at least ten minutes while we're here.'

'Hmf,' said Emily Lime, keeping her head resolutely *in* the book. 'I'll give your suggestion all due consideration. No. Now shut up and lead me to the nineteenth century.'

Daphne consulted the map she had picked up on the way in. 'Straight through here.' She pointed the way. 'Then turn left at the Rembrandt.'

George gave a nod, turned Emily Lime, still reading, to face the far door, then prodded her to set her walking blindly that way. He and Daphne followed behind, steering Emily Lime as necessary towards their destination.

Trouble was not yet brewing, but they passed signs that it had at least begun to simmer. Every gallery attendant they saw looked, at the very least, extremely anxious. One of them was shaking so much as a first former asked him to light her cigarette that the vibrations rattled the chandelier. They arrived in the Impressionists room too late to catch precisely what Gillian Fremsley had said about the naked lady in the tin bath in the picture she was pointing at, but judging by the shade of red that it had turned the attendant's face, they could take a reasonable guess. Next door, a Picasso etching was inspiring lively debate between a group of fifth formers. George didn't catch much of the conversation but the main points being discussed seemed to be: a) whether or not Picasso could draw properly if he wanted to; and b) who would win in a fight between him and Matisse.

'Do you think Miss Woolley's love of free expression extends to letting Amelia Covington climb up bronze statues of former prime ministers?' Daphne pointed through a doorway they were passing at Amelia Covington climbing up a bronze statue.

'Probably,' said George. Then in his best attempt at an impression, he continued: '*We must not deny the girls the opportunity of free physical expression, nor their right to political commentary through the medium of mountaineering skills.* I'm not sure the gallery staff agree, mind.'

Daphne caught a glimpse of a man in a suit approaching the intrepid climber. 'Hang on,' she said. 'I'll get a picture.'

George nudged Emily Lime to a halt.

'Are we there?' said Emily Lime without lowering her book.

'No. We're stopping off for a bit of sightseeing. Stay put, Lime.'

Emily Lime said nothing and flipped a page over as George lumbered after Daphne.

As George and Daphne entered, Amelia had just completed her ascent of David Lloyd George (1863–1945) and was attempting to raise herself from a kneeling position and stand up straight on top of his head. Daphne raised her camera.

'Hoy!' yelled the man in the suit. 'Stop that!'

Daphne took a half step backwards in an effort to keep Amelia in frame, which wasn't easy because she was wobbling so much. Then just as Daphne clicked the shutter a hand landed on her shoulder and spun her around.

'I said, stop that. Didn't you hear? Photography is strictly forbidden.'

'What?' Daphne looked amazed. 'Oh. Sorry. I *assumed* you were talking to the girl on top of the statue.'

'I'll come to her in due course. Once she comes down again I shall be having some *very* stern words with her, don't you worry. But in the meantime, as director of the gallery, I must insist that—' He reached for Daphne's camera, then as she pulled it out of his reach his face screwed up in pain. 'Ow!' he squealed.

Amelia Covington, back on floor level, had kicked him hard in the backside, and now sped off towards Italian printmaking of the sixteenth century.

'You little—' The man set off after her. 'No photographs!' he called back over his shoulder to Daphne, who must not have heard him as she took his picture.

'Good luck catching her,' muttered George. 'She's Sports Day champion for the hundred yard dash.'

George and Daphne set Emily Lime in motion again and guided her to a seat at the centre of the Nineteenth Century gallery.

'Comfortable on your throne, Your Majesty?' said George.

Emily Lime grunted and waved him away.

'Some culture, miss?' George said to Daphne, with an expansive flourish.

'Why, I don't mind if I do,' said Daphne.

'Righto, let's cram some in quick, before the barbarians arrive.'

It was a large room and, as yet, free of other St Rita's pupils, so as Daphne and George set about examining the paintings, the uniformed woman seated by the doorway set about examining them.

'No sudden moves,' whispered George. 'I think we're under close observation.'

'Oh yes. Maybe we'd better closely observe some art, then. You know, like well-behaved gallery goers.'

'You're probably right,' chuckled George. 'Who's this fella, then?' He pointed at the large canvas in front of them.

Daphne consulted the sign by its side. 'Joseph Mallord William Turner – crikey, that's a mouthful.'

'1775–1851,' called out Emily Lime without bothering to look up from her book.

'1775–1851,' confirmed Daphne. 'Oil on canvas.'

She stood back to join George who had adopted his best impersonation of an art lover, with one hand on his chin and an inquisitive eyebrow raised.

'Do you think he was in a hurry and didn't have time to finish it?' he said.

'No, I . . . I think it's meant to look like that.' Daphne squinted at it. 'It is a bit . . . fuzzy, though, isn't it?'

'Tch!' said Emily Lime. '*Turner's late work is characterized by an increasingly impressionistic technique, in which a sense of atmosphere is favoured over the rendering of detail. The effect of this bold approach, innovative for its time, is both powerful and profound.* Oswald Gilbert, *The Power of Art*, Trent and Hobson Press, 1936.'

'Well, that's maybe what Oswald Gilbert thinks, but you haven't even looked at the thing, Lime, so what do you know?'

'I'll have you know,' said Emily Lime, 'that I know a very great deal. I have read two books about Turner in particular, and sixteen other works of reference that comment on—'

'That's all very well,' said George. 'But I bet you didn't bother to look at the pictures.'

'The pictures?' Emily Lime looked up from her reading, insulted and aghast. 'I'm not an *infant*! I don't look at . . .' She trailed off, staring past George with a bemused expression. 'What's that meant to be?'

'Oh, this?' George poked a jaunty thumb in the

direction of the painting. 'This is powerful and profound is what this is.'

Emily Lime closed her book, rose, and walked across to join Daphne and George. She leaned in to examine the painting up close, then stepped back to take it in as a whole, frowning all the while. Then she read the sign. Then she looked at the painting again.

'It's very yellow,' she said.

They all gazed at it a little longer.

'Perhaps he was having an off day,' suggested Daphne.

The intrusive clattering of frantic feet behind them drew their attention away from art criticism.

'Ey up! She's gained a following, I see.' George pointed at Amelia Covington trotting through the gallery with a gaggle of huffing puffing staff in tepid pursuit.

Daphne raised her camera and took a surreptitious snap as they passed.

'And do you ladies wish to remain in the nineteenth century?' said George. 'Or shall we join the party in the Dutch gallery?'

Emily Lime had already pushed her nose back

into her book and offered no opinion, but Daphne gave a smile and nodded towards the door. By the time they entered, Amelia and her pursuers were long gone. Evidence of their passing remained, however, in the form of an attendant sprawled face down on the floor next to an empty pedestal, a vase in her outstretched arms. A dark-haired sixth former, a deeply unimpressed Cynthia Rawlinson and Mr Thanet were all staring out through one of the doorways.

'I think they went that way,' said George.

'Oh well,' said Daphne. 'I daresay I can catch them on the next lap.' She indicated her camera.

'You know you're not allowed to use that thing in here.' Cynthia Rawlinson's voice blustered into their ears from behind them. Daphne and George turned to face her.

'Yes, Cynthia,' said George. 'We are perfectly well aware. But luckily all the staff are too busy with middle distance running to do anything about it. And *ex*-head girls can't tell us what to do either, can they?'

A flicker of pain passed across Cynthia's face. It was there and gone in a moment, but George saw it clearly enough before Cynthia put her defences back up and unleashed a practised scowl on him.

'Well, just . . . just . . .' Words failed her and the scowl fell away. 'Oh, just . . . watch it, that's all,' she said weakly. She jabbed a finger half-heartedly in the air between them, then her head dropped and she wandered off towards the door they had come in by.

'Crikey,' said Daphne. 'I think she's broken.'

George stared after her. 'Blimey,' he muttered. 'Well, I, um . . . suppose we may as well . . .' He looked puzzled. 'Hang on. Where's Lime gone?'

A quick scan of the room revealed that Emily Lime, her head in her book, was shuffling slowly towards Mr Thanet in the opposite corner of the room. Mr Thanet, bent over and now closely examining a small painting, seemed blissfully unaware of her.

'Oh dear!' said Daphne. 'We forgot to put the handbrake on.'

'Oi, Lime!' shouted George, which drew the attention of the gallery attendant.

'Miss! Excuse me, miss!'

Daphne, George and the attendant were now all rushing towards the oblivious Emily Lime, still advancing like a relentless clockwork toy towards Mr Thanet.

'Lime, you deaf maniac! Stop!' yelled George. 'Before you—'

'Oh!' said Mr Thanet, as Emily Lime collided with his sticking out bottom, pushing him forward. His ankle caught on the low wire barrier that prevented visitors from getting too close to the painting. He teetered, arms flung back in an effort not to lose his balance, then inevitably began to fall forward, his face heading straight for the painting. 'Nyeurgh!' he said reasonably.

Then, just as it seemed inevitable that he was going to inadvertently head butt a 300-year-old work of art, he threw his arms forward, slammed one hand against the wall either side of the frame, and brought his face to a halt within inches of the canvas. He remained there for a moment, his body angled awkwardly across the gap between the barrier and the wall, face to face with the yellow bird depicted on the canvas.

'Oi!'

Mr Thanet took a breath, pushed off from the wall, and sprang back to an upright position.

'I will thank you, sir, to please behave yourself and set a better example to the young persons present in the gallery today!' The Dutch room's attendant had arrived behind Mr Thanet and was making a meal of looking huffily unimpressed. 'Lord knows they're bad enough to begin with, without any encouragement from their elders. You ought to be ashamed of yourself. That's one of the treasures of our collection, here. You could have been in a lot of trouble if you'd damaged that one.'

'Actually,' said George, 'it wasn't his . . .' He trailed off as he looked round for Emily Lime who was still obliviously reading and plodding off on a new trajectory. Daphne trotted after her and brought her to a halt.

'Sorry,' said Mr Thanet. Then he put his hand to his ear and looked puzzled for a moment.

'Well, you just watch yourself.'

Mr Thanet gave a vague wave of compliance

while he scanned the floor, then he crouched down and picked up a yellow pencil, before standing once more. 'Sorry,' he said again, and placed the pencil behind his ear.

'I should hope so. This place has gone mad today. Schoolgirls running riot, teachers trying to kiss the paintings . . .'

'I'm not actually . . .' said Mr Thanet rather distantly. 'And I wasn't—'

'What next? That's what I want to know. What next?'

And this is when Miss Cosgrove ran into the room.

'Fire!' she shouted, just as the alarm began to ring.

SIX

'Stop jogging my arm!' said Emily Lime. 'You'll make me lose my place.'

'For goodness' sake,' said Daphne, pushing her out of the door, 'close your book and look where you're going, can't you? We have to get out of the building. Can't you hear the fire bell?'

'Yes, I *can*!' said Emily Lime. 'And it's *very* distracting!'

Miss Woolley, ahead of them, ducked into a gallery off to one side. 'Everybody out!' she shouted. 'Come on, please, girls.'

A smattering of first formers scuttled out and off through the door that George and co. were heading towards.

'Put it *down*!' George tried to grab the book out of Emily Lime's hand, but she whipped it away out of his reach.

'Just let me finish this chapter. Would it kill you to be a little patient?'

'Yes! Quite possibly! Lime, this is no time to be . . . exactly like you always are. This is an actual, proper emergency. So will you please put the book down and hurry up and then maybe we won't all get burned to death.'

Emily Lime snapped the book shut. 'There. There really was no need to be so melodramatic. I doubt there's actually a fire at—'

Miss Woolley came back out of the opposite door and almost collided with them. Her face was smudged with soot. And there was a distinct whiff of smoke in the air. '*Out!* Everyone get OUT! NOW!'

A gallery attendant and a handful of St Rita's girls pushed past them and out through the door.

'You too, miss,' the attendant called back to Miss Deakins. 'Outside and assemble at the front of the building.'

'Is there anyone else left back there?' Miss Deakins pointed back the way that George and the others had come.

George and Daphne looked back while Emily Lime sauntered out.

'Erm, Cynthia's just coming.' George pointed to the ex-head girl approaching. 'And Mr Thanet *was* in there with us, but I haven't seen him come out.'

'And there was a lower sixth form girl too,' said Daphne. 'Dark curly hair, a little taller than me.'

'Oh yes, Molly Fox.' George glanced round. 'Mind you, we were busy steering Lime, so we might have missed them.'

Miss Deakins frowned, staring past them through a haze of smoke at the door to the Dutch room. She bit her lip. 'I'd better check. Now—'

'No!' Miss Woolley strode past them. 'I'll go. All of you, get out. I'll . . . I'll join you in a moment. See them out safely, Frances.'

'Yes, of course.' Miss Deakins stared after the departing head, then turned to the children. 'Come on, then. Calmly and quickly.' She held one arm out to her side and wheeled the other hand like a

policeman directing traffic, while shooting glances off in all directions.

They set off through the thickening smoke.

'Blimey!'

'Don't panic.' Miss Deakins fell into step behind them. 'On we— Miss Quirk, is that you?' She stopped again, staring off through a side door. 'This way, Margaret! This—' Worry pulled her face tight. She bit her lip. 'On you go, children, I'll be out— Stop that! This is no time for snapshots, girl!'

'Sorry, miss,' said Daphne, clicking the shutter once more at the receding figure of Miss Woolley.

'Out! Now!' Miss Deakins pointed the way, while herself dashing towards the side door. 'Margaret – Miss Quirk! We have to get out!'

In a moment she too had disappeared into a bank of smoke.

George and Daphne cast a worried glance after her but did as they were told, with George steering Emily Lime, and Daphne snapping a few last photographs as they made for the exit. Outside, they joined a large group at the bottom of the gallery steps.

'There must still be a lot of girls inside,' said Cynthia Rawlinson, patrolling the assembled crowd.

'Well,' said George, 'there's certainly a lot of the girls not here. But I reckon most of them went off into town. They're not in the gallery.'

'Miss Woolley and Miss Deakins are still inside, though,' said Daphne. 'And Miss Quirk. And I can't see Mr Thanet anywhere either.'

A girl emerged from the entrance and started down the steps.

'Oh, but there's that sixth former from the Dutch room.'

'Molly Fox,' said George. 'Oh, and here's Thanet now.'

The caretaker appeared from the gallery door and began an erratic descent.

'He's even more sooty than Miss Deakins was,' said Daphne.

George saw, as Mr Thanet drew closer, that this was true, and that the reason he was weaving about was that he had tears in his eyes. At the bottom of the steps the ground took him by surprise and he stumbled into George who caught hold and steadied him.

'You all right, Mr T?' he said.

'Oh. Sorry,' said Mr Thanet, clapping George on the shoulder. 'Got, um . . . smoke in my eyes. Must've taken a bit of a wrong turn on the way out. My eyes are . . .' He trailed off and pulled a handkerchief from his trouser pocket and wiped at his eyes, then turned to look anxiously back at the gallery. A wisp of smoke drifted from the doorway, then a figure emerged, backwards, hunched over, and moving slowly.

'Who's this now?' said Daphne.

Two members of gallery staff started off up the steps towards the figure, who managed one more laborious step out from the door.

'It's Deakins!' said George. 'And I think . . . Oh! She's dragging someone out!'

They watched as Miss Deakins came to a halt, released the wrists of the figure she had dragged out, then sank to her knees. At this moment the two gallery staff arrived at the top of the steps. While one took Miss Deakins' arm to help her up, the other lifted the prostrate figure onto his shoulders and unsteadily began a slow descent of the steps as smoke billowed from the door behind him.

Miss Deakins, coughing and breathing hard,

shook off her assistant's helping hand and eyed the crowd with intense purpose. She pushed a strand of hair off her face, smudging a patch of soot up her cheek as she did so.

'Where is everyone?' Her voice was urgent. 'How many are still inside?'

'We don't—' began George, but he was cut off by another voice.

'All the girls are accounted for,' said Cynthia, stepping forward. 'I've asked around and everyone who was in the gallery is here, except for Amelia Covington, who fled to the bus to hide from the gallery staff some time ago, and Marion and Cicely who went to call the fire brigade. Everyone else sneaked off into town. I can make you a list if you'd like?'

'No.'

Miss Deakins scanned the crowd, muttering to herself. 'Thanet, Quirk, Cosgrove. And Mrs Fotheringay is . . .' She glanced over to see the gallery staff helping the figure she had brought out of the building unsteadily to her feet. 'Thank goodness. Mrs Fotheringay seems to be all right. But . . .'

She shot frantic glances around the crowd, then

raised her voice to be heard above the din of the bells of approaching fire engines.

'Has anyone seen the head?'

'Oh!' said Cynthia. 'No.' Her face fell.

They all turned to face the gallery, thick smoke billowing from the doorway.

Miss Deakins' voice was shaky now. 'Where's Miss Woolley?'

SEVEN

'Who's in charge here?' said the fireman in a strong, clear voice as he strode up the steps.

A man in a suit, who Daphne recognized from their earlier meeting beside the statue of Lloyd George, raised a meek hand.

'Montague,' he said. 'I'm the director of the gallery. Um, I suppose that makes me . . .'

'Right.' The fireman ignored Mr Montague's offer of a limp handshake and instead stared up through narrowed eyes at the column of smoke emanating from the gallery. 'I understand that all members of gallery staff are accounted for, and none of the St Rita's pupils or other visitors are still in the building, but one member of St Rita's staff is still unaccounted for?'

'Yes,' said Mr Montague. 'I think, um, the head, Mrs um . . .'

'Miss Woolley,' said Cynthia Rawlinson, edging in closer to the fireman.

He nodded. 'And the fire is in a gallery in the western wing of the building?'

'Um, which way is west?' said Mr Montague.

The fireman dragged his eyes away from the gallery just long enough to give Montague a pitying look, then pointed. 'Left,' he said.

'Yes. West. Yes. The smoke seemed to be coming from Gallery Twenty-three, the Chinese room.'

'Thank you.' The fireman turned to his colleagues, nodded towards the gallery building and began climbing the steps two at a time, issuing instructions as he went. After a few paces a group of half a dozen men peeled off, running back towards the fire engines while the remaining officers broke into a run up the steps.

'Oh, good-o, they've arrived then?' Marion Fink galumphed to a halt next to George. Cicely sidled in beside her.

'Yuss,' said George, lost in thought. 'Hey, you were gone a long while. The phone box isn't *that* far away.'

'Ah no, well you see, we didn't have any change – nothing smaller than a fiver – so we had to go to a café to get some.'

'But you don't even need any money for a nine-nine-nine call. They're free.'

'Well, I know that *now*. Anyway, when we got through, it turned out they'd already sent some engines out, because someone else had called them before us.'

'Probably someone from the gallery. Not that

surprising that they beat you to it after all the bloomin' time you took.'

Marion looked indignant. 'Well, I'm jolly sorry if you think we let the side down, but we went as fast as we could. Cicely didn't even wait to finish her second teacake. Did you, Cicely?'

'Mm,' said Cicely.

'And they were jolly good too. It was quite the sacrifice.'

Before George had a chance to commend Marion on her selflessness, Daphne tapped his shoulder and brought his attention back to the firemen.

'The second team are going in with the hose now,' she said. 'I hope they'll be OK. It must be terrible in there. There's *so* much smoke!'

'It'll be a wonder if they can save the building by the looks of it.'

Daphne bit her lip. 'I just hope they can save—'

'Miss Woolley!' George pointed as a fireman stepped out through the smoke with the unconscious figure of Miss Woolley draped over his shoulder. 'Thank goodness she's out.' He blew out a breath and wiped a hand across his forehead, then jabbed an elbow into Daphne's ribs. 'Now, get some photos of the gallery burning down so we can definitely get her sacked.'

Daphne scowled disapprovingly, despite the fact that she was already lining up her next shot.

'It *is* rather beautiful, isn't it?' Miss Deakins nodded over at the twisting column of smoke. 'The way the sunlight catches it. It's like a living moving sculpture. Exquisite!' Her eyes glazed with wonder.

'I s'pose. Bit of a shame if the gallery burns down, mind,' said George.

Miss Deakins dislodged the rapturous expression from her face with a brisk shake of her head. 'Er, yes. Indeed.' She frowned purposefully. 'Quite tragic. Let's hope that those brave firemen can save it. And especially the abstract exhibition.'

She took one last wistful peek at the smoke, then turned her attention to the blackened and shambolic figure approaching them.

'Oh, thank goodness. Miss Woolley! Are you all right?'

Miss Woolley shifted a sooty tangle of hair away from her face while brushing away with the other hand Miss Deakins' efforts to support her. 'Don't fuss!' she snapped. 'I've had enough of that already from the firemen. Apparently I passed out, because of the smoke presumably. And I must have banged my head as I fell.' She winced as her efforts to rearrange her hair reached a tender spot at the back of her skull. 'But I am quite all right now, out here in the fresh air, thank you. Now, tell me, Miss Deakins: is everyone safe?'

'Yes, miss.' Cynthia Rawlinson butted in. 'Not everyone is *here*, but everyone is accounted for. I've asked around and made a list of the girls who went off truanting into town, if you'd like to see?'

'Truanting in town, you say? Then, yes, I certainly *would* like to see.'

Cynthia grinned and handed over a sheet of paper with names listed down it in her best handwriting.

'Admirable!' muttered Miss Woolley with a nod. 'These girls will have to be congratulated on their initiative.'

Cynthia's face fell.

'Oh, what's this now?' said Daphne.

More smoke than ever was bursting from the doorway of the gallery, but shadows were forming within that smoke, faint and nebulous at first, then darkening into figures, which eventually stepped out from the murk. The fire chief came first, carrying in each gloved hand a metal litter bin from which emerged a twisting pillar of thick smoke.

The next fireman to emerge carried another. These two placed the smoking bins on the ground outside the door. The chief summoned the man carrying the hose, then pointed to the bins. Then the fellow with the hose fired a sharp burst of water into each bin in turn, toppling each of them over, spilling smouldering ashes which were, in turn, also doused until only faint wisps of smoke traced their way upwards from the sodden remains. There was still some smoke escaping from the doorway, but it was more of a fine mist now, rather than the earlier storm clouds.

The fire chief picked up a bin and descended the steps. Appropriately enough, he appeared to be fuming.

'Whoever thinks that this is funny,' he said, throwing down the blackened bin, 'is sorely mistaken.'

'Funny?' said Mr Montague. 'I'm sorry, I don't understand.'

'*You* don't need to be sorry, sir.' The chief turned his attention to the assembled girls. 'But you can be quite certain that once I find out who was responsible for such a reckless waste of my and my men's time, I will make *them* very sorry indeed.' He eyed the crowd with a smouldering fury. 'Someone thought it would be a jolly wheeze to fake a fire in the gallery.'

'Fake? Oh, thank goodness!' Montague went a little weak at the knees with relief.

'Yes. Lots of smoke, but no fire. Or at least almost no fire. Just three bins in one of the galleries. It seems the culprit has used as yet unidentified chemicals to maximize the effect. I expect I'll be able to identify the guilty party in due course when we've examined

the residues. I *strongly* suggest, though, that whoever did this saves me the effort by owning up now.
That way we might be able to avoid the involvement
of the—'

'Police!' yelled someone at the back of the crowd.

'Yes, obviously,' said the fireman. 'But please
don't interrupt when I'm—'

'No,' said the voice from the back. 'I mean: *look!
Police!*'

Everyone turned to look, and there indeed were
two newly arrived vehicles: a police car, out of which
sprang Detective Inspector Bright of the Pilkington
constabulary, and a van, from the back of which
leaked an unsavoury stream of grumpy-looking
St Rita's pupils under the watchful gaze of a trio of
uniformed officers.

Inspector Bright approached the crowd,
searched amongst them with a purposeful glance,
then addressed himself to the head.

'Miss . . . Woolley, is it?' he said.

'Why, yes,' said Miss Woolley.

Inspector Bright pointed a weary finger back
over his shoulder at the surly individuals disgorging
from the van. 'I believe these belong to you.'

'Er, yes. That is to say, the girls are in my care as their headmistress. They are, of course, all free spirits who *belong* only to themselves.'

Inspector Bright eyed her levelly for quite some time, pursed his lips and gave a very small nod. 'Quite,' he said. 'Nevertheless, I'm returning them to you now. They're all here except for' – he consulted a notebook – 'Millicent Vane. You can have her back in the morning when there's a fighting chance she'll have sobered up. As for the rest of them, their most recent demonstrations of that free spirit you prize so highly have, sadly, involved the contravention of' – he flipped through a further three pages of his notebook, wincing occasionally along the way – 'four laws, twenty-nine byelaws and three Commandments. I must ask you please, in future, to confine their glorious free spirits very strictly to the grounds of the school.'

'But aren't you going to arrest any of them?' spluttered Cynthia.

'Well, miss,' said the inspector, eyeing her coolly. 'I'd really rather not. For one thing we don't have room for all of them in our cells. And for another, they'd be a terrible influence on our other prisoners.'

'Oh yes?' Cynthia sneered. 'And what about this attempted arson?' She indicated the gallery.

'Ah, yes. I had in fact applied my detective skills to the presence of the large red engines and accompanying officers of the fire service, and indeed the dissipating pall of smoke hanging above the gallery. But of course I would not wish to jump to any conclusions about the involvement of St Rita's pupils – however inevitable that might seem to be – without first assessing the facts of the matter.' He turned to the fire chief with a thin smile. 'Hello, Neville. Much damage done?'

'A hoax, Inspector,' said the fireman. 'No major harm, I think. No structural damage, anyway, just a bit of a mess. As you arrived I was just appealing to the better nature of the perpetrators to give themselves up.'

Inspector Bright tried, with limited success, to suppress a laugh. 'And, how did that go?'

'As well as you might expect.'

'Well then.' The inspector turned to the girls with a menacing stare. 'We'll take away these remains for closer examination, and no doubt in due course we'll pay St Rita's a visit – oh, joy – to make further enquiries.'

'But everyone is free to go?' asked Cynthia. 'I know the school has no standards of discipline, but I hoped at least the police might try to maintain some kind of order.'

The inspector gave her a hard stare. 'Oh, believe me, we do,' he said. 'It's a matter of priorities. And while the actions of your schoolmates are ... *vexing* at times, they are relatively minor in the grand scheme of things. So, please, all of you, get back on your bus and proceed, in an orderly and lawful manner, back to St Rita's. And stay there until after I've retired.'

EIGHT

Considering he had so recently made it clear that he never wanted to see anyone from St Rita's ever again, Inspector Bright's dramatic reappearance beside the bus came as something of a surprise. He sprinted into view, his overcoat flapping wildly, one hand raised above his head.

'Nobody move!' he shouted.

George paused on the step into the bus. 'Wasn't he just saying that we should all shove off?'

'More or less,' said Daphne, behind him.

'How are we meant to do that without moving? I

wish he'd make up his bloomin' mind.'

George stepped back down and turned to see an array of police officers and Mr Montague the gallery manager trotting towards them in the inspector's wake.

'Everybody, back off the bus!' commanded the inspector.

Miss Woolley appeared at the bus door. 'Have you relented, Inspector? May the girls resume their cultural enrichment now?'

'No,' spluttered Mr Montague, red-faced. 'But they can give back the *Canary*!'

'Canary?' George gave Daphne a puzzled look. Daphne shrugged.

'Perhaps,' said the inspector, in a rather calmer tone, 'it might be best if we all went back inside for a little chat.'

Even with a sizeable police presence on hand, it took quite some time to get the girls, gathered in the now more or less smoke-free Dutch room, to quieten down. Half the girls were throwing wild accusations at one another regarding who was to blame, while the other half were placing bets about it.

'I don't *want* to arrest you all for disorderly conduct,' yelled Inspector Bright, 'but I will if I have to. So please just settle down and with a bit of luck we can all get home in time for tea. I'm giving you all one chance. A painting is missing.' He consulted his notebook. 'Specifically the one that was hanging just *there.*' He pointed to a blank space on the wall. 'If whoever has this painting gives it back right now, then Mr Montague has, very kindly, agreed that you can be let off with a warning.'

He left a generous pause which no one chose to fill.

'If, however, we have to go to the trouble of searching you all, and your bus, and questioning you, causing us to work late, and become hungry and grumpy, then the individual responsible will be subject to the full force of the law, and indeed the displeasure of Constable Hawkins.'

At this point a police officer who resembled a grizzly bear that had been shaved against its will grunted to identify himself.

'This is not a threat I bandy about casually. Constable Hawkins is a fine fellow, but he doesn't like to miss his tea. And I believe tonight Mrs Hawkins is cooking sausages . . .'

Constable Hawkins emitted a low hum of longing.

'. . . which are his favourite. So in the interests of truth, justice and sausages, I implore you, whoever has taken the painting, please give it back. Or, if you know who has taken it, tell us.'

Inspector Bright paused again, and Constable Hawkins unleashed a brutal stare from beneath thick black eyebrows so forcefully knotted that it seemed unlikely they would ever again be disentangled. The girls (and George) cast accusing glances amongst themselves, and there were disgruntled mutterings aplenty, not least from Cynthia. But there was no confession.

'Very well then,' sighed Inspector Bright. He turned to his men. 'Sorry, lads, it's going to be a late one.'

Constable Hawkins, visibly fuming, led a small

team off to start searching the bus, while the inspector led Mr Montague out of the room. Then the sergeant and other officers herded the St Rita's girls to one end of the Dutch room.

It turned out that the first item on the sergeant's agenda was for all of the girls to be searched. This was no easy task, but it was nonetheless achieved with as much dignity as the handful of female police officers available could manage, and with as little cooperation as the girls could offer. The enterprise was not wholly fruitless, turning up as it did three knuckledusters, four flick knives and a hip flask of moonshine whisky, all of which were confiscated into police custody, but there was no sign of a small Dutch oil painting, nor any obvious clues to its whereabouts.

Then they searched Miss Woolley and the teachers – in a rather perfunctory manner and with likewise no success – and finally George and Mr Thanet. The young constable assigned to George seemed to be taking the whole rigmarole very seriously, silently patting down the sides of George's blazer. His hands came to a halt when they reached George's bulging pockets.

'What have you got in there?' he said, his nose wrinkling.

'Well,' began George, thinking hard, 'let's see . . . There's a small bag of sugar mice, a pencil, a piece of chalk, a yo-yo, a bit of string and a three-penny bit, I'm pretty sure. They're all quite near the top. But lower down . . . I'm blessed if I can remember. Might be a bit of fish or somesuch – I generally keep some in for the Beast – that's the school cat . . . What else?' He scratched his head. 'Shall I just empty everything out so you can see for yourself?'

The constable gave a reluctant nod and George knelt down and began to unload his pockets of their cargo.

It took a while.

When he'd finished George, still kneeling, surveyed the jumble of goods spread on the floor before him.

'Heck!' he said. 'It's a wonder it all fits in really, isn't it?' He looked up at the constable with a smile. 'Anything of interest to your investigation?'

The constable, his mouth tightly closed, shook his head.

'Anything you need me to explain?'

The constable shook his head again. He looked slightly alarmed, but George chose not to dwell on this.

'Or, um, identify?'

The constable, once again, indicated that his answer was no, while resolutely keeping his mouth firmly shut. And judging by the colour of his face he hadn't breathed through his nose for a while either.

'Probably just as well,' said George, frowning thoughtfully at something black and gelatinous near his right knee. He gave it a prod. It quivered unnervingly. 'I'd be hard pressed to tell you what a lot of it is. Or used to be.' He picked up the globule and gave it a sniff, winced, then held it up towards the policeman's face. 'Any ideas?'

The constable recoiled in horror, shook his head and fluttered a hand at the detritus on the floor.

'Oh, shall I put it all away again?'

The young constable nodded with manic enthusiasm.

'Righto,' said George.

While he set about the task of reloading his pockets, and the constable dashed off to a safe distance and fresher air, George glanced over at Mr Thanet who was at that moment in an animated whispered conversation with the sergeant. It seemed that he too had emptied his pockets for inspection but that in his case the police were taking more interest.

'Well, that's as may be, sir,' the sergeant was saying. 'But you must see that, under the circumstances, it does look, as we say in the police force, *a bit iffy*, doesn't it?'

'I'm the school caretaker,' hissed Mr Thanet.

'But not the *gallery* caretaker, sir. No good reason for you to have this here, is there?' He raised a hand in which he was holding Mr Thanet's screwdriver.

'No, of course not. It must have been in my pocket from the last time I used it which was . . .' Mr Thanet's face wrinkled in thought. 'Yesterday evening. I was fixing a lamp for Miss Quirk. Well, trying to, anyway.'

'Round about half past eight, wasn't it, Mr Thanet?' said George.

'Oh,' said the sergeant. 'So you witnessed this, did you, lad?'

'Oh no, Sergeant. But that's when all the lights went out, so . . .' He dropped his voice to a whisper. 'Electrics aren't Mr Thanet's strongest suit, to be honest.'

Mr Thanet looked aggrieved. 'It was an unusually complicated lamp,' he muttered.

'Anyway,' said the sergeant, 'let's go and have a chat with the inspector shall we, sir. If you'd like to follow me.' Then, whether he liked to or not, Mr Thanet followed him, as the sergeant gripped his arm tightly and led him away. As various of the girls shouted advice (mostly along the lines of 'don't tell 'em nuffink, Mr T!'), George rejoined Daphne and Emily Lime.

'Well, they're barking up the wrong tree there,' chuckled George, cocking a thumb toward the departing caretaker. 'I hardly see Thanet as a

102

cunning art thief, do you?'

'No,' said Daphne. 'But have you seen which painting is missing?'

George followed the line of Daphne's pointing finger to the bare space on the wall surrounded by a low wire barrier, with a policeman standing next to it.

'Oh!' said George. 'That was the picture that he was looking at.'

'Yes. Extremely closely, thanks to Emily Lime. And the attendant is hardly likely to forget that.'

'What was it anyway?' said George. 'In all the fuss I didn't exactly get a good look at it.'

'Nor me. Small painting of a bird, I think.' Daphne shrugged. 'And we can't get close enough to read the label on the wall now because the police won't let anyone near it. What did that man Montague call it? The Canary?'

'*The Fish Seller's Canary*, I should think' said Emily Lime without lowering her book. 'Oil on canvas, 1670, by Jan van Biergaarten, 1649–1720. Eight and a quarter inches by eleven and seven-eighths. On loan from the collection of Lord and Lady Chorley.'

George and Daphne looked at her, amazed. Or

rather they looked at the cover of the book that still obscured her face (*Going With the Flow: My Life in Fluid Mechanics* by Professor J. B. Kwang).

George pulled the book down.

Daphne said: 'How do you know all that?'

Emily Lime sneered. 'I read a book, obviously: *Dutch Masters of the 17th Century* by Gertrude Planck, Loughborough University Press, 1949; Dewey number: 759.94.'

'And you just remembered?'

'Yes. I have a good memory.'

'Huh!' George harrumphed. 'For things in books maybe. What's my middle name?'

'I have no idea. Why should I know that? It's a ridiculous question.'

'How about Daphne's middle name?'

Emily Lime went still for a moment, her face twitching more than usual in response to some frantic activity taking place behind it. She frowned and hummed and scowled and mumbled in thought. Then she gave up.

'No, you're going to have to tell me,' she said. 'Who's Daphne again?'

'Oh, for heaven's sake!' said George.

'Never mind that,' said Daphne (who minded quite enough for the both of them). 'This painting: did your book say if it was worth much?'

'Yes,' said Emily Lime.

'And is it?'

'No. According to the book, van Biergaarten was *an artist who never fully realized his early promise despite a brief apprenticeship in the studio of master painter Abel van Koestell (1628–1672). His best pieces are charming minor works principally of historical interest in relation to his more esteemed tutor.*'

George contemplated this. 'Five out of ten, must try harder,' he said.

'But in any case,' said Daphne, 'it's an odd painting to steal when there's a Rembrandt on offer that must be worth oodles more.'

'*Rembrandt van Rijn,*' said Emily Lime. '*1606–1669. Born in—*'

'All right!' said George. 'The point is, a proper art thief would choose something else to steal. It's a shame, mind. If a proper thief had stolen something worth a fortune then we could solve who did it and get a big reward again.'

'Yes,' said Daphne.

'But it looks like it's just one of our lot robbing a worthless painting of a dicky bird for a lark, which I reckon the police won't need our help to work out. And even if they did there'd only be a tuppence ha'penny reward.'

'Well, yes,' said Daphne. 'But it needn't be someone doing it for fun. It could have been a thief who just didn't know what he was doing – for instance, a school caretaker who could use a bit of extra money but who might not know what's what and just choose a small painting that was easy to get at.'

George looked shocked. 'You don't really think Thanet did it, do you?'

'Not really,' said Daphne. She frowned. 'But I *can* see why the police might.'

NINE

Emily Lime turned the final page of her final book, read it in no time at all, closed the cover, looked up, and frowned.

'Oh. We're still here?' she said.

George, who was lying on his back nearby, opened his eyes and raised his head to try out a withering look on her. Emily Lime failed either to notice or to wither.

'Yes,' said George. 'We're still here. We were here before, and we haven't moved. Why on earth would we not still be here?'

'I thought we might have moved. While I was reading. Why isn't Thanet driving us back to the school?'

'Because,' said Daphne, stretching her arms as if she had just woken, 'he's a bit busy being questioned by the police at the moment.'

'Still?' Emily Lime screwed up her already quite screwed-up face by an extra notch or two. 'Why is that man so slow at everything? They questioned me and it didn't take long at all.'

'Well,' said Daphne, 'you weren't much use to them as any kind of a witness, because you had your head in a book the whole time. They probably felt that Mr Thanet had rather more to tell them.'

'As their prime suspect,' said George. He gave his head a scratch. 'And they probably found him much less annoying.'

'I wasn't annoying actually. I was very helpful. I tried to tell them all about Jan van Biergaarten, but they weren't even interested, the Philistines. Anyway, why do we need Thanet to drive us back? I could do it. I've read two books about driving.' She paused. 'Or that little squirt from the second form, who was so good at parking.'

'I think,' said Daphne, with a touch of weariness in her voice, 'that Miss Woolley would prefer it if we were driven by someone with practical experience *and* a driving licence.'

'And who's tall enough to see over the steering wheel,' said George. He hauled himself up to a sitting position. 'Plus, obviously Mr Thanet is innocent and we wouldn't just leave him behind. Would we?'

'Why not?'

'Oh, come on,' said George. 'He's not much of a handyman, but he's a good sort. He wouldn't steal. And after you nearly broke his neck with that trip-wire in the library last term, I'd have thought you *might* feel like you owed him a favour.'

'After *we* set that tripwire,' said Emily Lime, 'that was meant for a bank robber. Thanet had no business creeping into the library in the dark like that. He should have turned the light on and looked where he was going.' She gave George a defiant stare. 'And anyway, he *didn't* break his neck, did he?'

'No,' said George. 'He had a concussion instead.'

'A *mild* concussion.'

'Oh yuss, a mild concussion when he arrived in the san. But it was severe by the time Matron had treated him. So I just think—'

'Here he comes now,' said Daphne.

And there, indeed, he came, somewhat bowed and shuffling along behind Inspector Bright. Mr Thanet looked tired and distressed.

'Did they duff you up, Mr T?' enquired a chirpy first former. 'Only my dad says if the rozzers duff you up you can sue 'em.'

Mr Thanet raised his head a little and shook it, much to the first former's clear disappointment.

By this time Thanet and the inspector had the attention of the whole room. Those who had been seated now stood, and those that had been racing around trying to do harm to one another were now still. All eyes were on Inspector Bright as he spoke.

'Right,' he said. 'We have, *as yet*, no grounds to take Mr Thanet or any of the rest of you into custody, so you are all free to—'

A tremendous cheer, with more than a smattering of jeering mixed into it, obliterated the rest of the inspector's words. There was also some spontaneous celebratory dancing from a couple of fifth formers who only moments ago had been locked in vicious combat. It took some moments for the tumult to subside enough for the inspector to continue.

'You are all—' He flapped his arms about in a 'calm down, for heaven's sake' motion while Constable Hawkins deployed a quieting glower. 'YOU ARE ALL,' the inspector yelled, and the girls' noise abated a little. 'You are all free to go, BUT' – he waved a very serious pointy finger in an accusatory arc that encompassed everyone in the room – 'our enquiries are ongoing. We have no proof that any St Rita's girl was involved in the theft of the painting, but since anyone else in the gallery with an ounce of sense had fled at the first sight of you, we have to consider the possibility very seriously indeed. We will be seeing you again before long, have no doubt. But for now: away with you all.' He made a shooing motion. 'Begone.'

Looking a little dazed, Miss Woolley began to usher the girls towards the exit and, with the help of the other staff and the robust encouragement of the police, they were returned to the bus with a remarkable lack of fuss.

'Are you sure you'll be all right driving,' George heard Miss Deakins asking Mr Thanet, who was slumped in the driver's seat, as she passed by him.

Thanet gave a glazed nod, rubbed a hand across his forehead and started up the engine.

As the last of the pupils settled into a seat, Miss Woolley stepped aboard, calling back over her shoulder to the gallery director: 'Yes, yes. I'll come back tomorrow and we can talk about it then, Mr Montague. But for now my main concern must be the welfare of the girls. So you must excuse me.'

She gave a pleading look to Mr Thanet, who flicked the switch to close the door behind her. Miss Woolley let out a silent sigh, turned as if to address the passengers, but said nothing. She stood there in still silence, her face worn blank.

'Er, shall I . . . ?' said Mr Thanet.

'Drive,' said Miss Woolley. 'Just drive.'

Then she collapsed into the seat behind him. And as they set off into the night, it seemed as if she was shaking. Though whether this was merely due to the vibration of the engine, it was impossible to tell.

TEN

'**B**reakfast,' said George as the library door creaked open to announce his arrival, 'is the most important meal of the day.'

Daphne, already fully dressed in her uniform and hard at work despite how early it was, said something in reply, but as she was kneeling down with her head in a shelf, George couldn't hear a word she was saying.

'I can't hear a word you're saying.'

Daphne removed her head from Anthropology and tried again. 'I said *it can't be the most important meal if I can't eat it.* And unless they've replaced that hopeless cook with someone far less likely to kill us all, then—' She sniffed the air. 'Hang on. What's that?'

She pointed at a large tea towel-covered tray that George, still in his pyjamas and dressing gown, set down on one of the tables.

'What, this?' he said innocently.

'Yes, that.' Daphne strode over, nose first. 'Is it . . . ?' Her face lit up with hope. 'Can it be . . . ?' She looked as if she was floating towards him now, borne aloft by some mysterious, rapturous magic. 'Is it . . . *toast*?'

With a flourish worthy of a magician revealing a newly conjured rabbit, George whisked away the tea towel, unveiling a plate piled high with toast. Next to it was a butter dish, a teapot, a jug of milk and sundry other items.

'Might be,' said George. 'Fancy a slice?'

Daphne sank into a chair, dropped her chin into her hands and gazed at it adoringly. 'I think it might be too beautiful to eat,' she said.

George served the uppermost thick slice of golden bready gorgeousness onto a small plate and offered it to Daphne. 'I bet you can manage,' he said.

Daphne was already reaching for the butter knife. 'I'll see what I can do,' she said.

A shout or three from George lured Emily Lime grumbling from her office and she joined them at the table, helping herself to two choice rounds without a word.

'You're welcome,' said George.

'I didn't thank you,' sneered Emily Lime.

'I noticed,' said George, adding a dollop of jam to his own toast, spreading it evenly over the lush, buttery surface, then dribbling a bright crimson smear of it down the front of his dressing gown as he took a greedy bite.

Then they were quiet until all the toast was gone. Or rather, none of them spoke. The eating of the toast – the sublime, delicious, exquisite toast – was a messy and noisy affair, involving loud chewing, sighs of pleasure, the occasional low moan and a concluding satisfied belch from George, but there were no words.

Afterwards, Daphne asked a question. 'How did you get that?'

George licked a smear of butter from a finger. 'Mmm . . . Miss Bagley got me to do a couple of chores for her yesterday, and I s'pose she must have been pleased with how I did 'em, because this morning she sorted me out that little lot as a reward. I got yesterday's *Pilkington Chronicle* off her too. I thought there might be something new on the robbery in it.' He passed the newspaper to Emily Lime who unfolded it and began to leaf through the pages.

'Crikey!' said Daphne. 'If ever Miss Bagley wants more chores doing and you're not available, then feel free to recommend me. That was . . .' Words failed her.

'That was *real food*,' said George.

'Yes! Thanks so much for sharing, George.'

'You're very welcome,' said George. He looked over to Emily Lime, mechanically turning the pages of the newspaper and scanning through them. 'And you're welcome too, Emily Lime.'

'Hmf!' said Emily Lime, and the top of the newspaper fluttered in the breeze of her disdain.

George rolled his eyes. 'Anything 'bout the robbery, then?'

'A few lines on page twelve. *Ongoing lines of enquiry ... Police making every effort ... Unwavering determination to solve the case ...*'

'That's good,' said George.

'No, it's not, you dunderhead!' said Emily Lime. 'That's what they say when they haven't got a clue! It's been nearly a fortnight now and it sounds like they haven't got any solid evidence at all.'

'Well, exactly,' said George. 'So hopefully they won't be bothering poor old Mr Thanet any more.'

'And, if they're getting nowhere,' said Daphne, 'then maybe *we* could investigate a bit. You know, for . . .' She trailed off as she squinted out at the playing fields with a puzzled look. She stood and wandered towards the window.

'We haven't had any parcels in the post lately,

have we?' asked George.

'Um . . . no, I don't . . .' Daphne reached at the window and frowned. 'I . . . don't think so. Why?'

'We've got one today.' He pointed to a brown paper package on the tray, half-covered by the tea towel. 'And, mmm . . . Miss Bagley said *another parcel for you* when she handed it over.'

'How . . . odd,' said Daphne distractedly. Standing right by the window now, she stared out with a perplexed look, absolutely still and speechless for a moment.

'You all right, Daffers? What's up?'

She pointed out of the window and said: 'Cows!'

'*Cows?*' said Emily Lime. '*Cows* are up? What are you talking about?'

'Cows!' said George, who had joined Daphne at the window and added his own pointing finger.

Emily Lime stomped over to join them. 'What on earth is wrong with you both? I sometimes think—' Her mouth dropped open as she too pointed out of the window. 'Cows?' she said.

'Cows,' said Daphne.

'Cows!' said George.

Cows. There were cows in the playing field, over

near Mr Thanet's cottage, about twelve of them, chewing at the grass in a contented manner.

'Either St Cuthbert's have made some odd selections for their hockey team this year,' said George, 'or someone left the gate open to Farmer Sterne's field.'

They looked across from Mr Thanet's cottage to where woodland turned into a shabby barbed wire fence, and then along a little further to where a five-bar wooden gate hung open.

'Oh dear,' said George. 'In which case, Daffers, we'd best get out there and persuade those cows back into their field before old Sterne finds out.' He started towards the door.

'Us?' Daphne's voice betrayed a distinct lack of enthusiasm for the project. 'Why should we ...?'

'Because Farmer Sterne is not the biggest fan of St Rita's as it is, so I reckon it's best if we sort this out before he notices. And before anyone gets any ideas about putting roast beef on the menu.'

'But, I mean ...'

'Come on.'

George led Daphne to the rear door of the school. They stepped out, flinching as the cold slap of the air hit them, the frosty grass of the playing field crunching beneath their feet.

'Oh, look! They're beauties!' said George. 'Old Sterne may be a miserable old grump, but he knows his cattle, I'll say that for him. Not many folk keep Belted Galloways this far south. We're very lucky, seeing them up close.'

Daphne made an odd sort of noise in reply that suggested she did not fully appreciate her good fortune.

They came alongside the nearest of them, away from the main group chewing at the grass near the centre of the hockey pitch, and George gave it a friendly slap on its flank. Daphne kept her distance.

'Hello there,' said George in a low, warm voice, as the animal raised its head and cast him a curious glance. 'What are you doing out here, eh? Come for a holiday, have you? Might not be such a good spot for you, to be honest. The creatures in our school aren't such gentle beasts as you.'

'Are you sure they're gentle?' said Daphne.

'Oh yes,' said George, smiling as the cow nuzzled its head against his chest. He inclined his head towards the nearby main group and he and the cow set off that way. 'They'll be just fine, so long as we keep our voices calm and quiet and we don't surprise them with any sudden movements.'

'Moo!' bellowed a distant voice behind them.

George looked over his shoulder and saw a scattering of girls, many still in their nightclothes, racing across the field towards them. They did not look likely to keep calm or quiet.

'Oh, blimey!' said George, turning to face them. He tried to think of a way to persuade the oncoming horde to stop without making too much noise himself. He heard the crunch of frost-hardened earth beneath hooves as the cattle began to mill uneasily around him. One mighty beast rounded to face the approaching girls and its flank knocked George sideways into Daphne who let out a squeak of surprise.

'George!' Daphne's voice was little more than a whisper, but it crackled with fear. The cattle surrounded them now, huge and restless. If they took fright, it wouldn't matter how gentle their nature was, their mass and their strength would be dangerous, possibly deadly. George tried to catch the eye of the girl at the head of the approaching group but could barely see over the hulking body of the cow that stood in his way. He raised his hands slowly above his head and gestured for the girls to stop. But they trampled on, giggling and jeering, as the cattle shuffled into agitated motion.

Daphne yelped as one cow lumbered into her sideways. It was only a gentle blow but still it was enough that she lost her balance and fell to the ground. George twisted round to check she was all right and saw her already climbing to her feet, flustered but unharmed. When he turned back to the girls, he saw that one was advancing ahead of the others, her dressing gown held like a bullfighter's cape out at her side. The cow nearest to George looked up and gave her a curious look.

'Oh, please don't . . .' muttered George.

'C'mon, moo cow,' said the girl. She gave the dressing gown a provocative swish. '*Toro! Toro!*'

'Don't be daft, Marjorie.' George made his voice as loud and as forceful as he dared. The cow buffeted George as it faced Marjorie with a sharp snort. George regained his balance, raised a hand, threw Marjorie his most pleading look . . .

And she stopped. She dropped her dressing

gown, and she came to a dead halt. In fact, all the girls stopped. They did not move, they did not speak, they stopped smiling too, stared instead with rapt attention in George's direction, as if he had perfectly communicated the gravity of the situation and left them humbled and ashamed. The cows around him stopped jostling, all the tension of a moment earlier magically lifted away.

George was amazed. He had had no idea that he commanded such authority, but it was a very welcome surprise to learn that—

Oh, wait.

Of course he *didn't*.

He realized that the girls weren't looking at *him*; they were staring right past him. He turned to see what it was that had so captured their attention.

It was a man with a gun.

Well, thought George, that makes a lot more sense.

ELEVEN

'Why have you got your hands up?' asked Daphne as she clambered to her feet.

George gave a nod in the direction of the angry-looking man pointing a shotgun at them.

'Oh!' said Daphne. She put her hands up.

'You trying to steal my animals, boy? Missy?'

'No, Mr Sterne,' said George. 'We saw they'd got loose and we were going to put them back for you.'

'Oh, yes? And that was going to take all of you, was it?' He gave the shotgun a wiggle to indicate the crowd of other girls, causing a ripple of fear to pass through their ranks.

'Honestly?' said George. 'I wouldn't want to guess at that lot's plans. Probably a rodeo. But we were just trying to help, honest. Wouldn't want these beauties getting spooked by that lot. They're Belted Galloways, aren't they?'

'Aye.' The farmer examined George thoughtfully. 'Well, I suppose you 'int exactly dressed for cattle rustling.' He lowered the gun. 'You know cattle, boy?'

George straightened his dressing gown. 'A little bit. Mostly just from books, and some things that . . . someone told me when I was little.' George looked away, remembering something distant. 'Anyway, I just like 'em.' He gave the farmer a smile.

'Oh yes?' Sterne raised his gun again and motioned for George and Daphne to extract themselves from the herd. 'Well, you can just save up your pocket money and get your own then, can't you? And leave mine be. That cat o' yourn's bad enough, scarin' my herd. Lucky I only give it a warning blast to scare it off, it was. If I see it in my field again I'll give it both barrels. 'An' the same'll go for you lot if you 'int careful. Now, g'wan!'

George and Daphne did as they were told and picked their way out from among the cows, then joined the rest of the children.

'At least we know why the Beast's disappeared,' muttered George. 'You all right, Daffers?'

'Er, yes, I think so.' Daphne's voice quavered. 'Just a bit of a fright. Well, two frights: first the cows, then the shotgun. This sort of thing never happened at my old school.'

'Blimey!' George smiled. 'What kind of an

education is that? You needn't have worried, though. Old Sterne likes to act fierce, but I'll bet that gun's not even loaded.'

They both looked over at the farmer who had lowered the shotgun now and was patting the rump of one of the cows as he urged it to set off back towards the gate.

With Sterne's attention on the cows, the other girls relaxed a little. Some began to chatter to each other, some started to drift back towards the school. Marjorie, standing just behind George, muttered darkly that she didn't appreciate having a shotgun pointed her way.

Sterne gave the nearest cow's flank a hearty thwack. The cow continued chewing contentedly at the hockey field grass. 'G'wan, you lazy beast, shift yourself!'

'I'll get it moving for you,' muttered Marjorie.

George turned and saw her, posed like an archer with one hand raised straight out in front of her, the other pulled back. Between the two was the tense elastic of her catapult.

'No!' said George. 'Don't!'

But she did.

Her fingers twitched open, the elastic snapped forwards, and a small pebble flew hard into the flesh of the cow's rear.

'Bullseye!' said Marjorie, with a flagrant disregard for anatomical accuracy.

The cow bucked in pain, and crashed into Sterne's chest, sending him toppling backwards, arms flailing in a doomed effort to regain his balance. He fell backwards, hit the ground hard, and—

BOOM!

There was a deafening explosion as the shotgun went off, both barrels, harmlessly into the air. The children froze in shock at the sudden noise, but the cattle were set into frenzied motion, jostling and colliding, building panic within the tightly grouped herd, until they charged, all together, straight towards the horrified audience of St Rita's pupils.

'Stampede!' someone yelled.

'Run!' screamed another.

George looked to Daphne, found her terrified face looking straight back at him, saw her set off sprinting after the other girls. He heard the rumble of hooves approaching too loud and too fast.

He ran.

It was a sound plan, except that George was no good at running. Whereas the cows turned out to be surprisingly athletic. Within seconds they were all around him, their hooves drumming a thunderous rhythm.

'Oh, heck!'

Now the cows seemed terrifying rather than magnificent, and there seemed to be hundreds of them rather than a dozen. He swung his head wildly from side to side as he ran on, trying to match the pace of the cows and looking for some faint possibility of escape. But there was no way out. He was right in the midst of them.

'Oh, lumme!'

One cow barged past him on one side then another buffeted him back the other way. He stumbled, a cry rising in his throat, terror filling his heart, and the wild, wide eyes of frightened cattle seemed to swim around him. He knew he was panicking, but he could not help himself. His heart and mind were racing. Another collision almost felled him, bent him over, half turned him around.

'Oh no!'

He looked into a vista of trampling hooves. Directly in the path of one powerful beast, he made to jump out of the way but felt his foot slip on the frosty grass, began to fall again, arms thrown up to the heavens.

'NO!'

Then, miraculously, he felt a tightness around one wrist, felt himself lifted off his feet, twisted in mid-air. For a moment he was weightless. The thundering hooves and all other sound fell away and George floated, staring up at the crisp grey blue of the beautiful winter sky. So beautiful. So, so beautiful.

Then he landed hard on his back. Something

heavy hit his chest and everything went dark.

If he had been trampled to death, George thought, then it hadn't hurt as much as he would have expected. Although, now he came to think of it, if he *was* dead, then presumably he wouldn't feel anything at all now. And he did. His arm felt like it had been wrenched almost out of its socket, his back ached and his chest hurt. He couldn't work it out at all. He could hear, a little way away, Farmer Sterne talking softly to his cows, calming them, and altogether saying things less softly to some St Rita's girls who hadn't yet fled back inside. Then he felt a weight lift from him, and the dark receded and formed into the shape of Mr Thanet standing above him.

'Sorry,' said Mr Thanet. 'Are you all right?'

George sat up and tried to work out the correct answer. His chest hurt a bit less now that Mr Thanet wasn't lying on top of it. And he was increasingly confident that he wasn't dead. Not even slightly.

'Yuss,' he said. 'Fine, ta.'

He rubbed a fearless hand through his hair and looked around to assess the state of things. Here's how it stood: Farmer Sterne was a short distance away with half a dozen of the cows, which were huddled together and seemed now to be calm and content again, and happy to investigate the relative merits of the grass at the edge of the lacrosse pitch compared to that of the hockey pitch, which they had sampled earlier. The rest of the animals were more widely dispersed around the field, with one or two still on the move and agitated, but not enough to be a worry. All seemed reasonably calm.

'Thanks, Mr T,' said George. 'That could have been a bit sticky if you hadn't—' He turned back round to face the caretaker, but found Daphne there instead, her face full of worry. 'It's all right, Daffers. *I'm* all right.'

'Just about,' she said. 'But let's get you back in a nice safe library now.' She held out a hand to help him up.

'No. Ta. You go ahead. I need to have a word with Mr T.'

Daphne looked at him doubtfully.

George forced a smile. 'Really, I'm fine,' he said. 'Go on, you get in and I'll be with you in a bit.'

Daphne looked at him, appraising him coolly.

Then not so coolly jumped when one of the cows took a pace towards her. 'All right, then,' she said, stepping backwards and glancing between George and the cow and back again. 'But don't be long.' She turned and sped away.

A sharp cry of 'Hey!' alerted George to the fact that Mr Thanet was now striding over towards Farmer Sterne, looking determined and purposeful. He'd never seen Mr Thanet look determined *or* purposeful before, let alone both at the same time.

Sterne turned, looking no less angry than Thanet sounded.

'Now don't you go shouting your head off and riling up my cattle again.' Sterne stabbed the air with a finger. 'I've only just about got 'em calmed down after them little horrors sent 'em on the rampage.'

'Well, maybe you should take more care to keep them on your own land then!' Mr Thanet had got his finger out now, poking his own bit of air as he spoke. It looked a little as if the two of them were about to start duelling.

'Oh, don't you go sayin' it was me as let the bloomin' cows out. It was one o' them rotten girls,

as well you know. Sneakin' about, up to no good, an' without the common sense to close a bloomin' gate behind them. I've a good mind to call the police on 'em. There's a lovely clear footprint in a cowpat just by the gate there. Reckon one o' them detective fellas could soon work out who it was. After all that trouble at the gallery the other day, I reckon the police wouldn't think twice about locking 'em up for trespassin', an' . . .' Farmer Sterne paused as he set his keen legal brain to work. 'An' attempted cattle rustlin',' he said. 'An' the reckless endangerment of livestock.'

'Well, be my guest,' said Mr Thanet. 'You call the

police and tell them you think one of the girls might have left a gate open. And I'll tell them about you shooting at them.'

Farmer Sterne's finger froze in the air, mid-jab, while he considered this. His face rearranged itself thoughtfully.

'Well, seein' as 'ow I don't actually have a telephone, I s'pose I'll leave it this time,' he said at last. Then he redirected his pointy finger to indicate all points of the playing field. 'Now, give us an 'and gettin' these buggers back in their field, will ye?'

'All right,' said Thanet, without enthusiasm. He rubbed a hand across his face which now, drained of its earlier anger, looked tired and weary. Then he lumbered round to the side of one of the cows, gave it a gentle slap on its flank with one hand while gesturing forwards with the other, like a doorman showing a guest into a grand hotel.

'Tch.' Farmer Sterne shook his head. 'A lot of use you're gunna be, I can see.'

Thanet gave another half-hearted slap, which the cow responded to by mooing loudly in his ear. Thanet winced.

'Whassa matter, boy?' Sterne grinned. 'Bit

delicate this morning, are you? I seen you down the pub last night with some o' them teacher folk. You have one too many, did you?'

'My birthday,' Thanet croaked. 'I probably should have come home earlier but they kept buying me drinks. It was . . . a bit late by the time I got back.'

'Oh, you don't want to try to keep up with them teachers drinkin'.' Sterne gave a hefty thwack to the rump of another cow and set it in motion. 'They're devils for it. Mind you, I can't say as I blames 'em. You'd need a drop or two to keep you goin' teachin' in that school o' your'n.' He looked at George. 'No offence.'

'None taken,' said George. 'Can I help?' He indicated the scattered cows.

Mr Thanet gave him a doubtful look. Farmer Sterne gave him a *really* doubtful look. But then he said: 'Go on, then. You can fetch that daft 'un from over in the far corner there. But mind you be calm and quiet.'

Luckily the cow in question proved cooperative and it was a simple matter to lead it over to Farmer Sterne and Mr Thanet who by then had gathered the rest of the herd together and were encouraging them back towards the gate.

Farmer Sterne looked over. 'Well, blow me, look at you,' he said. 'Ain't you the cowman, eh? Reckon that 'un's taken to you, lad. Must like the smell of that dressing gown or summat, I reckon.'

The cow, as if to prove Sterne's point, nuzzled into George's side then licked his face.

'Gah! Gerroff!' said George.

'See, you're a natural.' Farmer Sterne shook off his smile. 'Now, g'wan back inside with you before you catch your death. You too, Mr Caretaker. You're worse than bloody useless anyway.'

Mr Thanet seemed to consider for a moment contesting this foul slur upon his cow-herding skills, then gave half a wave and a grunt and stepped towards George. George gave a grateful smile, then shivered as the cold air reminded him that he was dressed only in pyjamas and a dressing gown, all of which were wet.

Mr Thanet looked him up and down, shaking his head. 'Are you sure you're all right?'

'I'm grand, Mr Thanet,' said George, though his voice quavered. 'It was a good job you came when you did, though.' He grew quieter as he thought

139

back: the noise and the smell of the cows charging past him. 'It *was* a bit—' All of a sudden, George looked up towards Mr Thanet, who he saw now was lunging towards him with his arms outstretched. For some reason his face had gone fuzzy, but George could see that his mouth was moving. And he could hear a sound, like a voice underwater, and a long way off, but he couldn't make out any words. And he could see that there were snowflakes drifting down past his eyes, bright and blurred, while the rest of the world faded. Beautiful snowflakes, dancing in the air, while everything else went dark . . .

darker . . .

black . . .

Later, though it was impossible to tell how *much* later, a word formed in the warm, grey, cosy fuzz inside George's head.

'Here.'

George parted his eyelids cautiously, allowing in a general ambience of flickering orange and the sight of something white that was too close to his face to focus on. He pulled his head back, strained his eyes, and eventually made out a large white enamel mug, dented and chipped, hovering in the air before him.

'Tea,' said Mr Thanet from somewhere behind it. 'I guessed at three sugars.'

George gave a good hard blink as his brain tried to make sense of things. 'Close enough,' he said. 'Ta very much.'

He swallowed a hearty slurp of the strong, sweet tea, then took in his surroundings. He was sitting in the one armchair in the snug little sitting room of Mr Thanet's cottage. His dressing gown was draped over the fireguard, standing at an angle to the fire itself so as to allow most of the light and heat out into the room. As George's mind cleared, he thought back, identifying a hungry gap in his memory, after the cow business and before the not quite sweet enough cup of tea.

'Um,' he said, 'did I . . . faint?'

'Yes. Delayed shock, I think.'

'Oh.' George stared into the fire for a moment. 'Anyway,' he said, 'I should probably be getting back to the—'

'Finish your tea.' Mr Thanet's voice was quiet but firm. 'Then we'll make sure you're steady on your feet. After that, I'll find you a coat to borrow and walk you back to the school.'

'Don't take me to Matron!'

'I wouldn't dream of it.' Mr Thanet padded over to the door. 'I'll see if I've any biscuits left. Help get your strength back.'

'Ooh, ta.'

Alone in the sitting room, George looked around a little more. It was a cosy room. There were some unsteady-looking shelves in the alcove next to the fireplace with a few books, a wireless and a couple of framed photographs; there was a simple wooden chair as well as the worn but comfy armchair he was sitting in; there was a small low table covered in clutter partly concealed by yesterday's newspaper; and hanging on the walls, a smattering of framed pictures. At first, George noticed only the cracks in the walls emanating from the nails from which the pictures hung, but then he took in their subjects, just as Mr Thanet returned.

'Last two,' said the caretaker, handing over a plate with two slightly-the-worse-for-wear digestives on it.

'Ta,' said George, then waved a hand at the pictures. 'You'd better watch out, Mr T. If the police find

out you like bird pictures so much they'll likely have you back for questioning again.'

'Eh? Oh, yes, I suppose it wouldn't look too good, would it?' Thanet gave a weak smile.

'Not very,' said George through a sputtering of biscuit crumbs. He saw off the last of his tea and offered back the empty plate and mug. 'Ta for those. Done me the world of good, they have.'

'You're very welcome.' Mr Thanet took the plate and balanced the mug on top of it, where it promptly began to rattle.

'Hope you've not got anything too dangerous to do today with your hand shaking like that,' said George. 'Have you got delayed shock too?'

'Ha! No. Although I did get a real shock yesterday afternoon. Maybe it's the after-effect of that.' Mr Thanet lifted the mug from the plate and held it in his other hand.

'Round about quarter to five? When the lights went out again?'

Mr Thanet gave a thin smile.

'Another lamp, was it?'

'No. I was hanging a picture for Miss Deakins and managed to hit a wire with the nail.'

'Oof! That must have hurt.' George winced in sympathy.

'Oh, it's not so bad,' said Mr Thanet. 'You get used to it. Although looking at the painting was a bit painful. Very modern and . . . stripy. Anyway, never mind me, how are you feeling now?'

George stood up experimentally. 'Fit as a fiddle,' he said, wobbling only slightly.

Mr Thanet eyed him warily. 'All the same,' he said, 'I'll walk you—'

'No need. Bet you're busy enough already, aren't

you?' George had already gathered up his dressing gown which he found was now warm and wet rather than cold and wet.

'Well . . .' Mr Thanet considered the matter. 'At least wrap up warm.' He glanced out of the window. 'The snow's coming down hard now.' He opened the door and followed George out into the narrow hallway. Thanet nodded at an overcoat hanging on the bannister. 'Borrow that,' he said. 'Get it back to me when you can.' He carried on down the hall to the kitchen, calling back over his shoulder. 'Take a hat too. Under the stairs.'

George pushed aside a curtain to reveal an alcove beneath the staircase, with jackets, coats and hats hanging from hooks above shoes, wellingtons, a tool box and a shopping bag. Reaching for a cap from the furthest hook he managed only to knock it loose and it fell into the shopping bag. Then reaching to retrieve it, he stopped short as he caught sight of the bag's contents.

The sound of mugs and a plate joining other crockery in a washing-up bowl drifted from the kitchen.

George stared into the bag, breathless, his mind

racing. That was definitely the corner of a gilded wooden picture frame he could see. But surely it couldn't be . . .

He hooked a finger into the top of the bag and prised it open a little more for a better look.

'You know,' said Thanet emerging from the kitchen. 'I—'

'Got to dash!' said George, throwing his dressing gown into the bag and grabbing its handles. Turning his back to Mr Thanet as he pulled the bag out, he reached for the coat from the banisters and hurried for the door. 'Important library business. Thanks. Bye.'

He awkwardly opened the door, and launched himself outside, out into the falling snow, marching quickly away, working the too-big coat onto one arm and waving goodbye without looking back, gasped clouds of panic dotting the air in his wake.

Luckily for George, the time it took him to change out of his pyjamas meant that the trio of police officers heading for the playing field had already passed by when he re-emerged from the school's rear door.

'That one, is it?' said one gruff voice.

George stared after them as he eased the door quietly shut behind him.

'Yes.' The reply was weary and sad. George recognized Inspector Bright from his voice and his overcoat. 'Across the playing fields. But I don't think—'

George didn't catch the rest. He watched them marching across the grass towards Mr Thanet's cottage.

'Oh, lumme!' he said.

He ducked into the bike shed and selected a suitable bike, then stuffed the shopping bag into its basket as he wheeled it out, past Miss Cosgrove's motorbike and into the light. Out on the path he gave one last glance back at Inspector Bright, flanked by the other police officers, knocking at the cottage door then, grimacing, he climbed onto the saddle and pedalled determinedly away.

TWELVE

'Where have you *been*?' Daphne called up to George before the library door had even finished creaking shut behind him. He looked down at her, took in Emily Lime sitting at a nearby table with Hulky, and the absence of anyone else in the place. This was not much of a surprise to him as he'd had to negotiate his way back past pretty much every other girl in the school (plus Miss Cosgrove) having a snowball fight outside.

'I, er, had a cuppa with Mr T,' said George. 'And then I had to get changed. And then I, um, had to nip into the village, to the post office.'

'Well, you might have let us know.' Daphne looked exasperated. 'We were worried about you.'

'I wasn't,' said Emily Lime without looking up.

'*I* was worried about you,' said Daphne. '*And* you missed all the excitement!'

George descended the steps, brushing clods of snow from his coat as he went. 'More excitement? I think I've had enough for one day, ta. But what was it? Has Lime come up with *another* new system of shelving?'

'Actually—' said Emily Lime.

'No,' Daphne interrupted. 'Mr Thanet has been arrested!'

'Ah, yes,' said George. Then, when Daphne looked puzzled: 'I mean, oh no!'

'Apparently the police received an anonymous tip-off that he'd stolen the painting, and took him away *to help with their enquiries*. They searched his cottage too, but they didn't find anything.'

'No, well, they wouldn't . . .' muttered George.

'Eh?'

'Er, because obviously he's innocent, I mean.'

Daphne gave him a curious look, then seemed

to remember something. 'Anyway, um, now you're back perhaps you can help me out with . . . In here.' She led him to the office and, with a nervous glance back at Emily Lime, ushered him in.

'This thing you want me to help you with,' said George as Daphne followed him in and closed the door behind her.

'Yes?' said Daphne.

'Is it anything to do with the cow?' He pointed to the cow that was chewing at some paperwork on Emily Lime's desk.

'Yes,' she said. 'Good guess.'

'Why have you brought a cow into the library, Daffers?'

'It's part of my recruitment drive to encourage new readers.' Daphne rolled her eyes. 'Obviously I didn't bring it in. I was tidying up a while ago, and when I heard the door open I assumed it was you coming back. Then when I looked up I found *this* at the bottom of the steps.'

George gave the cow a friendly pat and it looked up at him from its papery meal. 'So you hid it from Lime in here?'

'I thought she might not approve.'

'Possibly not. But why didn't you just take it back out?'

'It's not easy to persuade a cow up stairs, you know. It didn't want to go, the silly lump.'

'Aw, don't call it a lump.' George patted the cow's snout. 'You're beautiful, aren't you?'

The cow licked George's face.

'Ew, that's disgusting!'

'Gerraway with you,' said George. 'I don't mind.'

'I didn't mean for you,' said Daphne. 'I just don't want the cow to get ill.'

George flashed her a poor imitation of having had his feelings hurt. 'And now I suppose you want *me* to get it out?'

Daphne shuffled her feet and gave a nod. 'Yes, please,' she said.

'Well, all right, but you'd better get Lime out of the way.'

'I'll lure her into Applied Maths,' said Daphne, opening the door. 'Give me two minutes.'

'Perfect.'

And so, two minutes later, George and a surprisingly cooperative cow made a break for it, past a slightly confused-looking Hulky. Then, twenty minutes after that, George returned alone.

'Did you . . . ?' whispered Daphne.

'Kind of,' said George. 'I had to take the long way round the fields, but I managed not to get spotted. Everyone's so intent on braining each other with snowballs that nobody even noticed us.'

'Well done.'

'But there was no way I could get to Sterne's field unseen so I've parked the cow in the woods for now, tied up out of sight. I'll get her back to the farm later. There's no rush, he's not too good with numbers once he runs out of fingers so he won't notice it's missing. Now, um . . . can I have a word?

In the office?'

'What is it?' Daphne scowled at the chewed-up paperwork on the desk as they entered.

'You know the police were told they'd find the stolen painting at Thanet's cottage?'

'Yes.'

'The only reason they didn't find it there,' said George, 'is because I did.'

'What?' cried Daphne, then clamped a hand over her mouth. 'So he *had* stolen it?'

'No. At least, I don't think so. It was in a bag under the stairs. And he told me to go in there. He'd have to be pretty stupid to deliberately send me looking for a hat where he knew he'd stashed stolen art.'

'Maybe,' said Daphne. 'But it *was* there.'

'Yuss, but . . . No! He's not a thief. I just know it. Besides, it was screwed to the wall in the gallery. Have you seen him using a screwdriver? I don't see him managing it without being noticed. And probably badly injured.' He gave his head a scratch. 'Come to think of it, I don't see how anyone could. But especially not Mr T.'

'Hmm . . . not exactly conclusive proof, but I see what you mean. And what have you done with the painting?'

'I posted it to the police station. That's why I went into Pelham. They'll have to let him go when it turns up first post tomorrow.'

'Maybe,' said Daphne. 'But they'll still want to find out who did steal it. You *did* wipe all your fingerprints off it, didn't you?'

George's face froze. He looked down at his fingers, then back up at Daphne. 'Oh,' he said. 'That would have been a good idea.'

Daphne looked up at the ceiling and let out a long slow breath. Then she looked at George. 'Oh, George . . . Well, I suppose all we can do now . . .'

'Yes?' said George.

'Is work out who actually did it before the police arrest you.'

'Good idea,' said George. 'How do we do that?'

'I haven't a clue,' said Daphne. 'But let's start with a look in Mr Thanet's cottage.'

THIRTEEN

'So you see,' George said to Emily Lime as they marched across the playing fields, picking their way between the last remaining skirmishes of the snowball fight, 'someone obviously tried to frame Mr T by planting the painting in his cottage and then telephoning the police.'

'Or even more obviously,' said Emily Lime, 'he really was the thief and he's just stupid.'

'No!' George scowled at her. 'He's definitely not a thief.' He opened the gate to the tiny garden at the front of Mr Thanet's cottage. 'That's handy. They can't have shut the door properly after they arrested Thanet. Look, it's open.'

He breezed in, and promptly tripped over a boot lying on the floor.

George recovered his balance and turned to see Daphne pointing at the boot's twin lying in the corner of the door frame. 'And that's *why* the door didn't shut properly,' she said. 'This was in the way.'

They moved inside.

'And what, precisely, are we looking for?' said Emily Lime.

'Evidence that someone else has been in here,' said George, stepping through to the sitting room.

'Someone else besides Mr Thanet, you and three policemen who seem to have turned the place upside down already?'

They all took in the general state of chaos in the room, then Emily Lime spotted that there were books scattered about the floor and, humming happily to herself, began replacing them on the wonky shelves.

'Maybe this is foolish,' said Daphne. 'If there were any clues to be found, then the police will probably already have taken them away.'

'Not necessarily,' said George, thinking painfully. 'They were looking for the painting. We're looking for . . . something else.'

'Ye-es . . .' said Daphne. 'But it does make it hard looking for something when we don't know what it is.' She examined a couple of the pictures of birds on the wall. 'And these don't help.'

'No. I know,' said George. He started to search through the bits and pieces on the table, lifting up the newspaper to reveal a mess of papers, and sundry other items beneath. 'Pipe, matches, some bills, a shopping list, a pencil sharpener and two pencils,' he said. 'Nothing helpful. If only—'

'Hang on.' Daphne stepped across to join him and picked up the pencils. 'I think...' She examined them closely, then held them up to George. 'Yes. See?'

George didn't see at all.

Daphne rolled her eyes. 'You are a terrible detective!' she said, and held up one of the pencils. '*This* is a standard issue St Rita's pencil. The same as we use in the library. Yellow. The same as Mr Thanet always has tucked behind his ear. Whereas I've never seen him' – she held up the other pencil – 'with a *blue* one. And look: it's been sharpened with a *knife*. Mr T only ever uses a sharpener.' She waved the yellow pencil again.

George nodded. 'You're right,' he said. 'He'd probably lose a hand if he used a knife. But if that's not Mr T's pencil, then whose is it?'

Emily Lime looked round from the bookshelf. 'Let me see that,' she said, and without waiting for a response snatched the pencil from Daphne's hand, examined it closely for a second, then took a notebook from her pocket. She opened the book and zigzagged the pencil point across a page. 'Soft lead,' she said, with a distinct tang of disapproval. 'An *artist's* pencil.'

'What kind of pencils do they use in the art room?' asked Daphne.

'I wouldn't know,' said George. 'I try to avoid going in. Arty crafty types are not to be trusted.'

'All the more reason to take a look, then,' said Daphne. 'The sixth formers have art at the moment, don't they? Why don't we drop in?'

'Well, we could, but we'll need an excuse.' George scrunched his face in thought.

'Oh, I've got an idea about that. Come on.' They made for the door. Daphne looked to Emily Lime to ask her if she was coming too but found she had returned to rearranging books. 'I'll explain on the way,' Daphne added.

'Righto.' They stepped out into the cold air. George lowered his voice. 'And can we detour through the woods? I just want to check on Myrtle.'

'Myrtle?'

'The cow.'

'You've given her a name? George, you *are* going to take her back to Farmer Sterne, aren't you?'

'Course.' George stared straight ahead as he led Daphne round the side of the cottage and into the woods. 'Eventually,' he muttered.

Twenty minutes later, approaching the art room, George was in a grump.

'It was an accident,' said Daphne, not for the first time.

'No one's that bad at throwing a ball,' said George. 'You deliberately chucked it out into the snow so I couldn't find it.'

'I did not. And anyway we have more pressing matters to attend to than playing with your cow.'

George grunted sulkily.

'I'm not even sure that cows can learn to fetch.'

'Of course she can. She's very gifted. You were just doing it wrong.'

Daphne stopped outside the art-room door, looked at George and considered saying something, then decided against it. 'Now, remember the plan?' she said instead.

'Yuss.'

'All right then.' Daphne pushed open the door and they slipped inside.

'Really, Molly?'

Miss Deakins was peering over the shoulder of one of the girls in the art room. George couldn't see the art mistress's face as he and Daphne slipped in at the back, but he could take a good guess at her expression from her tone of voice.

'*Drawing?*' she said. '*Observation?*' Her voice dripped with distaste. '*Realism?* It's all very . . . *literal*, isn't it?'

George shuffled after Daphne into the room and tried to ignore the attention they were attracting from some of the other girls, working less intently, or not at all, at their own easels.

'So disappointingly old-fashioned,' said Miss Deakins.

Nudges and whispers alerted more girls to George and Daphne's presence, and they variously winked, leered and pouted at George as they turned to look at him.

George began to wonder why it suddenly seemed so hot in the room. And what was that smell? It wasn't actually unpleasant in itself, but it reminded him of games lessons at his previous school for some reason, and his memories of Mr Peterson the games master were never happy ones.

'Look, miss!' A tall girl raised a long paintbrush in George's direction, flourishing it like a conductor's baton. 'I think the models have arrived for our life class.'

George's face burned hotter still.

'Oh, I say!' said another girl. 'Don't put the thought in my head, I'll have nightmares.'

'Now, girls,' said Miss Deakins. 'Don't be unkind.' Her voice was sharp now, with a deft authority that stopped the girls' laughter instantly. She raised an eyebrow in George's direction. 'Can I help you . . . George, isn't it? And Daphne? The detectives from the library? What can we do for you?'

'I, um . . .' George shuffled on the spot. 'That is, we—'

Daphne sighed and cut in. 'Sorry to disturb your class, miss.' She stepped in front of George, cutting him off from a particularly mischievous pout aimed at him by a blonde at the front. 'You recently requested a book from us on the subject of Paul Klee.'

'Oh, yes, and you sent along just the thing. Thank you. Not that the fifth form could appreciate him, I'm afraid. Do you need it back?'

'Oh no, not at all.' Daphne tiptoed towards Miss Deakins, her step as light as her voice. 'But it rather drew our attention to how inadequate parts of our Art section are. And our colleague, Emily Lime, is such a stickler for keeping up to date.'

George shuffled forward to stand beside Daphne. 'Er, yuss. But you see, the problem is that we just don't know enough about, er . . .'

'We lack the expertise,' said Daphne, 'in the more modern art movements. So we would very much value your suggestions as to what new books we should obtain.'

'If you can spare the time, like,' said George.

'Well, that would be my pleasure.' Miss Deakins beamed.

'And if it's not too disruptive, we'd like to ask your class too. I know Miss Woolley is very keen on listening to the will of the pupils.'

'Yes, of course,' said Miss Deakins, sounding as if she valued her pupils' opinion much less highly herself. 'Ask away.'

'You've got a pen, I s'pose?' said George, offering up one of the sheets of paper he'd brought along. 'Or a pencil?'

'Yes, thank you.' Miss Deakins took the paper. 'Now do please continue with today's exercise, girls,' she called out to the class. 'Write down your suggestions as quick as you can. Don't let this little diversion interrupt the flow of your inspiration.'

George and Daphne set off among the girls, distributing the sheets of paper.

'Yuss, just pop your . . . name on the top there . . .' George handed a paper to a pouty blonde as gingerly as a zookeeper feeding a tiger.

'And the title of any book you'd like to suggest, or an artist or an art movement that you feel is under-represented at present in the library . . .' Daphne dished out another couple.

Miss Deakins, meanwhile, continued to hold forth

from her desk in the corner as she compiled her list.

'So remember, girls: your task is to capture the *truth* of our little tableau here . . .' She gestured to an uninspiring selection of objects arranged on a table at the centre of the room. On top of an old newspaper were a rusty bucket, a cup and saucer, a lemon and a watering can. 'Not their *physical* appearance.' She cast a withering look at Molly Fox, the girl she had been speaking to when George and Daphne had arrived. 'But rather their *essence*, the fundamental truth of them, the very *soul* of them!'

'The soul of a *lemon*?' whispered Daphne.

'Lemon soul!' replied George, and Daphne giggled.

'Here, you see in my own interpretation how I have avoided the obvious responses.' Miss Deakins held up a painting which was almost entirely black, except for a scribble of grey and a wonky clod of murky yellow. 'I'm sure you'll all agree that, though I say so myself, it is every bit the equal of that fusty old daub that was stolen from the gallery!'

The muted response from the class suggested that, in fact, they didn't agree at all, but Miss Deakins either failed to notice or didn't care. She turned the painting round and took a fresh look at it herself, holding it at arm's length and studying it for several seconds. Then she smiled and carried it over to the side of the room.

'I think I'll hang it on the wall, to help inspire you.'

George and Daphne exchanged a glance, then set off back round the class, gathering up the papers.

'Thanks. Thank you. Ta very much.'

'And Miss Deakins?' Daphne smiled a bright, perky smile at the art mistress and held out a hand.

'Of course,' said Miss Deakins, holding up three sheets covered in dense, hurried scrawl.

Daphne took them and turned for the door. 'Well, do feel free to send any further thoughts along later, but we will take all these suggestions into account when we put in our next order. Thanks so much.'

'Yuss, ta.' George yanked the door open and waved Daphne through; then, ignoring the girl blowing him a mocking kiss, he quickly followed.

'Well, they nearly *all* had blue pencils.' Daphne's voice was filled with hushed excitement. 'But—'

'But hardly any were sharpened with a knife,' said George. 'Just two out of the girls on my side of the room, in fact: Dorothea Canning and Geetha Amin.'

'And only one on mine,' said Daphne. 'The girl whose drawing Miss Deakins didn't like, Molly Fox.'

'So, we have three suspects who use the same kind of pencil as the one we found.' George tapped his chin thoughtfully. 'But which one broke into Thanet's cottage and tried to frame him?'

'Hang on!' said Daphne. 'We haven't even proved *anyone* was in there, let alone that it was one of those three. And even if it was we can't just assume that they left the painting under his stairs.'

George waved away these ridiculous objections, mostly because he had no answer to any of them.

Daphne grabbed his arm and brought him to a halt. 'You can't just ignore these things, George,' she said. 'I want Mr Thanet to be innocent too, but wanting it isn't enough. We need to look at the evidence coolly, and accept what it tells us. If you go assuming things just because they're what you want to believe then you'll end up putting your foot in it.'

George scowled at her, then a thought struck him. '*Putting your foot in it!*' he said, and smiled a big wide smile. 'I've had a brilliant idea!'

'Oh dear,' said Daphne.

'No, really. This is proper brilliant.' He glanced out of a window. 'Oh, but maybe it's already too dark to—' He set off along the corridor, at what by his standards was quite a pace. 'Meet me in the library after breakfast tomorrow,' he called back over his shoulder, still grinning. 'I'll bring a clue.'

FOURTEEN

It took George quite a while to open the door to the library. His hand was frozen, and he was shivering, which made it difficult to grip the handle. When he eventually staggered into the room, there were only five people in there: Emily Lime, Daphne, Hulky and a pair of second formers, who were just leaving. They brushed past, casting anxious glances at him. George clumped stiffly down the steps into the body of the library. Emily Lime and Daphne hurried towards him, each wearing a concerned expression.

'Heavens, George! Are you all right?' said Daphne.

'Don't you *dare* touch any of the books!' said Emily Lime.

Daphne pulled out a chair at one of the study tables and George toppled stiffly onto it. The jolt dislodged a clump of snow from on top of his head and it fell to the table with a pillowy thump.

'Oh, for heaven's sake!' Emily Lime turned back round and made a beeline for the office. 'I'll get a cloth. Do *not* drip while I'm gone.'

Daphne, with scant regard for the perils of dripping or her own safety, brushed the remaining snow from George's head. George faintly noticed that she recoiled slightly at the touch of his hair, but he put this down to the shock of the cold. Daphne looked out of the tall library windows at the blizzard-like conditions outside.

'Crikey!' she said. 'I hadn't realized it was coming down so hard this morning. You must be freezing!'

'I-i-it is a b-bit . . . f-fresh, yuss,' said George. He had his right arm wrapped round his chest, hugging himself for warmth. Daphne looked down at his left hand, hanging down by the side of the chair, wrapped around the handles of a stout cloth shopping bag.

'What's in the bag?' she said.

'Evidence,' said George, managing a tight smile. There was a worrying crunching noise as he turned his head stiffly, first one way then the other. 'I t-tried to get it . . . yesterday b-but it was too d-dark to find it so I h-had to go out again . . . this morning. And then it was c-covered in snow so . . . it t-took . . . ages to f-find it.'

'I thought I told you *not* to drip,' squawked Emily Lime, returning with a bucket, a cloth and an old tea towel. She set to mopping up the melting snow from

171

the floor and handed George the tea towel. 'Dry yourself with that. Don't catch a cold and expect to get out of your duties. I won't have it.'

'Your sympathy, w-warmth and compassion are m-much appreciated,' George said sarcastically, though he was genuinely grateful for the towel.

Daphne glanced at it as George gave his hair a rub. 'You can't use that,' she said. 'It's absolutely filthy.'

'So is he,' said Emily Lime, and neither George nor Daphne could fault her logic.

A minute or so later and the floor, the table and George were all more or less dry, the bucket was a quarter full with murky water, George's hair had found a new way to be untidy, and Daphne had declared the tea towel a health hazard that ought to be encased in lead and buried for a thousand years. And George had warmed up enough to be pleased with himself. He lifted the shopping bag onto the table.

'What's this?' Emily Lime eyed the bag suspiciously.

'Evidence,' said George, and reached into the bag and pulled out of it a large, frozen-solid cowpat. He tapped it gently on the table top to demonstrate its rigidity. '*Hard* evidence!' He laid the cowpat flat on the table, brushed away a few flecks of snow and pointed at it. 'See! Totally frozen overnight.'

Daphne looked confused.

Emily Lime looked furious.

'It's a footprint,' said George. 'You see?'

'It's...' said Emily Lime. 'It's...' Her face struggled to find an appropriate expression. 'It's ... POO!' she said at last.

'Well, yes, obviously it's poo,' said George. 'But it's poo *with a footprint in it*!'

'But *whose* footprint?' said Daphne.

'That's precisely the point!' said George. 'This excellent cow pancake was just inside the gate to

Farmer Sterne's field. He was convinced that who-ever trod in it was the same person who left the gate open and let his cattle out. Now, Mr Thanet was out at the village pub last night for his birthday with some of the other staff. My guess is that someone broke in while he was out, planted the stolen paint-ing in the cottage, but when they left they spotted the light on in the library because Lime was working late, as usual, then took a detour into Sterne's field to avoid being seen. Then they trod in the cowpat, and luckily for us, it froze.'

'Luckily for us?' said Emily Lime, shaking with rage as she stared at the cowpat.

'That's right!' said George. 'It's a beautiful clear print.'

Daphne, unlike Emily Lime, did look. 'Actually,' she said, 'that *is* quite clever. Oh, and there's a crack across the sole.'

'Ooh,' said George, 'I hadn't noticed that. That'll make things easier.'

'So if this matches any of our three suspects' shoes . . .' Daphne's voice was infected with George's excitement now.

'Then we can work out which one of them was in

Thanet's place,' said George.

'Don't think that *I'm* having anything to do with this idiocy!' said Emily Lime.

'No need,' said George. 'I've had another brilliant idea. Daphne and me will deal with the idiocy without you.'

He started off towards the door. He got halfway before he returned, sheepishly grabbed the cowpat and the shopping bag, muttered, 'Evidence,' and then sloped off again with Daphne following behind.

'That told her,' said George as he pulled open the door.

'Yes,' said Daphne. 'Yes it did.' They stepped through. 'I'm just not entirely sure what.'

FIFTEEN

For reasons George did not explain they took a diversion to the school kitchens, then doubled back to the changing rooms.

'The sixth form have games now,' said George. 'We can sneak in, find the pegs with the girls' names on, and check their shoes. Easy-peasy, pudding and pie.' He slowed his pace for a moment and a faraway look took hold of his face. 'Pie!' he said.

'Do try to concentrate, George!' They were at the door to the changing rooms now and Daphne kept her voice low. 'Do you think they'll all be gone by now?'

'You'd know better than I would, Daffers. Funnily enough they're not keen on me changing with the girls. But I think we should be safe on that score. Miss Trowel likes 'em to get a move on, I hear. The only problem is Trowel herself. I had hoped, with the weather so bad, that she'd be torturing the girls in the gym. But as you can see' – George jabbed a thumb at the window in the gym door opposite – 'they're not there. Which means she's probably seen that it stopped snowing all of five minutes ago and thought it was fine to send them out on a cross country run, and she could be anywhere. Normally she heads to the staffroom for a brew, so we *should* be fine. But you'd best nip in and check, just to be on the safe side.'

'Me?' Daphne didn't sound delighted at the prospect. 'Thanks a bunch, George.'

'Go on, it'll be fine,' he whispered, opening the door. Daphne chucked him a frown and tiptoed in.

A moment later she reappeared at the door and beckoned George in, silencing him with a finger pressed to her lips. Inside, he squinted in the gloom as he tried to take in the unfamiliar surroundings. There were windows high up along one wall, but so

small and filthy and halfway covered in snow that barely any of the light from outside could fight its way in. Once his eyes had adjusted to the darkness, George looked to Daphne. She pointed to a door on which a plain wooden plaque read: *Games Mistress: Miss E Trowel*, then gave an exaggerated shrug and pressed her finger to her lips again. George gave a nod of understanding. Then each began their search on opposite sides of the room.

George found Dorothea Canning's clothes almost immediately. St Rita's being the school it was, every last garment had a name sewn into it in some form or another. The *D Canning* embroidered very clearly inside the collar of Dorothea's blouse was easy to read even in the murk. Kneeling to examine the corresponding shoes, George let out a breath he hadn't known he'd been holding when he saw that the soles were intact. He took a moment allowing his disappointment to settle, then continued along the line of pegs.

He turned to check on Daphne's progress. She was already halfway along the opposite wall and happened at that moment to be kneeling to examine a pair of shoes there. He turned his gaze away from her upturned bottom and waited for her to stand before tiptoeing over, noting the slump of her shoulders as he did so.

'No luck?' he whispered.

'No. Geetha's in the clear. You?'

'Dorothea,' he said, and shook his head. 'Haven't found Molly Fox yet, though.'

'Nor me,' hissed Daphne. 'Come on, we'd better get a move on.'

George scooted back to his side to continue the search. 'VW . . .' he muttered to himself, examining the label in the collar of the next shirt. 'Veronica Wiggins. Blimey, you could grow potatoes in there.' On to the next. 'Pasco, no. Khan, no. Now what is that meant to say?' He squinted at a pair of minuscule letters sewn in red thread, then unable to make them out, lifted the blouse from its peg to take it into better light.

He hadn't seen the hockey stick beneath it, propped against the wall, but he heard it clearly enough once it clattered to the floor. He shot a horrified look at Daphne, then, as one, they turned their heads to the door of Miss Trowel's cubicle.

'Who's there?' The voice was urgent and authoritative, unlike Daphne's and George's both of which, it seemed, had disappeared.

They stood there, frozen and silent as the cubicle door began to open. George had just the presence of mind to cast aside the blouse, flukily landing it back on its peg, before Miss Trowel appeared from the door looking athletic and alert, muscles tensed, like a big cat ready to pounce upon its prey.

'George?' Miss Trowel's stance softened and she pulled the door gently shut behind her. 'What on earth do you think you're doing?'

'Sorry, miss. I just knocked over this hockey stick,' said George, unnecessarily lifting the stick from the floor in illustration.

'That's *what you have done*,' said Miss Trowel. 'Which is not what I asked.' She turned her attention to Daphne. 'And you. Blakeway, isn't it?'

'Yes, miss,' said Daphne, who suddenly found herself standing up very straight indeed under Miss Trowel's narrow-eyed gaze.

'So, what's going on here? I didn't have either of you down as petty thieves.'

'Oh, no, miss,' said Daphne, sounding genuinely horrified at the idea.

Miss Trowel frowned, as if trying to remember something, then gave a little nod and turned to Daphne with a piercing stare. 'No. I remember now. You came to us last term under something of a cloud, I recall. An incident at your last school. But it wasn't theft, was it?'

'No, miss.' Daphne shuffled uneasily on the spot.

George, meanwhile, noticed for the first time that Miss Trowel had something in her hand. Seeing him looking, the games mistress whipped that hand behind her back with suspicious speed, but it was too late. George had seen what it was, and he knew it gave him an edge.

'Any good, miss?' he said, nice as pie.

'What?' Miss Trowel's voice had just a speck of panic in it.

'The *book*, miss. In your hand, miss. That you were *reading*, miss.'

He noticed out of the corner of his eye that Daphne's eyebrows had shot up.

'Any good, is it?'

'Actually, I . . .' Miss Trowel, even in the poor light, was visibly flushing. '. . . I wasn't actually reading it. I'd just . . . found it, on the floor, and I was just checking if there was a name written in it so I could return it to its owner.'

'Oh, I see,' said George. 'Most people do that on the inside of the cover, miss. Or on the title page maybe. You might want to try looking there first. Rather than on a page halfway through, like where you've currently got your finger. But, of course, you wouldn't know about that sort of thing, would you?'

Miss Trowel looked at him with a stony expression. 'No,' she said firmly. 'As well you know, games mistresses do not read. So you would be mistaken if you thought otherwise, and foolish to say such a thing to anyone. But, George, I know you would never leap to any mistaken conclusions. Just like I know that there must be a perfectly good explanation for you and Blakeway being here. And so long as you leave right now *and never speak of this again* I shall have no need to ask what that is.'

She looked at George. George looked at Miss Trowel.

'Deal?' said Miss Trowel.

'Absolutely, miss,' said George, already speeding for the door.

'Thank you, miss,' said Daphne, likewise scooting.

Back out in the corridor they slumped against the wall, side by side.

'Miss Trowel is a *reader*?' said Daphne. 'Is that even allowed?'

'She'd be drummed out of the Games Teachers' Guild if word ever got out,' said George. 'That'd be her career over.' He shook his head. 'I think she had more inside that little room of hers too.'

'Really?'

'Yuss. She pulled the door shut sharpish, but she had a comfy chair in there with a couple of books on the arm.'

'Crikey! Could you see what they were?'

'No. But I think the one in her hand' – George scraped a hand through his hair, thinking back to check his memory wasn't playing tricks on him – 'looked like . . . *poetry*!'

'No!'

'Honest!'

Daphne shook her head and smiled. 'Miss Trowel!' she said. 'You are a dark horse!' Then the smile dropped away. 'But what do we do now about Molly Fox's shoes?'

George considered this as they began to walk. 'We'd best lay off for a bit,' he said. 'Besides, we know Dorothea and Geetha are in the clear now, so we can assume that the only one left is our intruder. Molly Fox framed Mr Thanet.'

'Hardly,' said Daphne. 'Does she even have a motive? Why would she want to get Mr Thanet into trouble?'

George gave this some thought. 'Why would anyone?' he said. 'I mean, everyone moans about his work, obviously. He's a bit useless, but everyone likes him well enough.'

They had arrived back at the library. George pondered the matter as they climbed the steps, then as he pushed open the door a thought struck him.

'You know who might know?'

'Who?' said Daphne.

'Mr T himself, of course. We'll visit him and ask.'

'You mean . . . in prison?'

'Yes,' said George.

'No,' said Emily Lime.

She was standing at one of the study tables looking up from a large art book lying open before her. To her side Hulky sat in painful concentration with a book of her own.

'And why not?' said George, clumping towards her.

'Because he won't *be* in prison. They'll just be holding him in a cell at the police station for now. Haven't you read *any* of our books on criminal justice?'

'No. They look really boring. Well, we'll go to the police station then.'

'And you think they'll let you march straight in to talk to their prime suspect, do you?'

George gave his head an intrepid scratch. 'I dunno. Won't they?'

Emily Lime sighed and closed her book. 'No, of course not. Not unless you're very clever about it. And you are *not* very clever.'

George wrinkled his nose at this but made no objection.

'So it's just as well,' said Emily Lime, 'that I am.' She started towards the door with a purposeful stride. 'Come on!'

SIXTEEN

'Actually,' said Daphne, as Emily Lime led them past Pilkington's imposing prison building, 'I'm glad we're not going in there, but surely this isn't the way to the police station either.'

'Lime has a plan,' said George.

'Which is?'

'Blessed if I know,' said George. 'Hey, Lime, what are we doing?'

'We're getting authorization,' said Emily Lime.

'What kind of authorization, exactly?'

'Books, of course!'

They turned a corner and there before them stood the Pilkington Town Library, a Victorian redbrick building just a little taller than the shops and offices that surrounded it and sitting slightly further out on the pavement, as if proudly puffing its chest out. Emily Lime adjusted her beret and strode towards it.

'Brace yourself,' said George. 'I've been here with Lime before.' A frown of remembrance took hold of his face. 'It didn't end well.'

Ahead of them Emily Lime barged through the door in a manner that reminded Daphne of a gunfighter entering the saloon in a cowboy film she had once seen.

George and Daphne followed her in and found her standing next to Geology shaking her head.

'Don't start,' hissed George.

'But it's just so . . . *shoddy*!' said Emily Lime, pronouncing the word as if it had gone mouldy.

'It's not your library though, is it? They get to run this place their way, and you run the St Rita's library – heaven help us – your way. They don't tell you how to do it, so—'

'But it's chaos!' whispered Emily Lime.

George looked about the place, and at the mostly elderly readers quietly choosing books, perusing the newspapers, studying, reading or, in one case, sleeping quietly.

'Oh, yes,' he said. 'Proper bedlam, this is.'

'Tch.' Emily Lime rolled her eyes, reached down and picked out a geology book, then replaced it two places to the left. 'Precious metals in 553.8?' she said. 'It's a disgrace.'

'Oh, yuss,' said George. 'It's a wonder no one's marching in protest about their flagrant disregard of the Dewey Decimal System. Once we sort out this whole art robbery business we can inform the police about that as well. But for now, can we just find the books we need sharpish and get out before—'

A shadow fell over them all. 'Can I help you?'

'Oh, lumme!'

The three children turned and looked up at the tweed monolith who had addressed them.

'George,' said the monolith, bowing her head in his direction by precisely half a degree. 'Miss Lime,' she continued, with a less flamboyant nod in Emily Lime's direction. 'And I don't believe I know you.' She kept her violently unblinking eyes fixed on

Emily Lime and raised one finger a fraction of an inch to indicate Daphne.

'This is Daphne Blakeway,' said George in as close to a cheery tone as he could muster. 'Daphne, this is Cordelia Scruton, head librarian.'

'Scruton.' Emily Lime, standing absolutely still, stared lightning and high explosives straight into her eyes.

'Lime.' The towering presence stared an icy gale direct from the Arctic wastelands straight back at her.

The air crackled between them. (Or perhaps that was George farting nervously.)

'We need some books,' said Emily Lime.

'Oh, really?'

George wondered when either of them might blink again.

'If you can even *find them*.' Emily Lime pursed her lips. It was a tiny movement, barely visible to the human eye, but at the same time immensely provoking. 'In this *madhouse*.'

'If I can't find them' – Cordelia Scruton raised her eyebrows by a hair's breadth – 'it will be because *this* library has readers come into it, some of whom *borrow* books. If you were a librarian – oh, I beg your pardon, an *assistant* librarian – in a *real* library, you might be familiar with this behaviour, rather than only seeing one illiterate barbarian a week when she wanders in by mistake while searching for the lavatory.'

It was odd, George thought, because usually Emily Lime blinked all the time. She was a very blinky girl.

'Or else,' went on Miss Scruton, 'because whatever squalid volume you wish to see is of no interest to our superior readers.'

'Like the man with the cheese crumbs and brown

sauce in his beard?' said Daphne.

Cordelia Scruton frowned, then blinked, then frowned because she had blinked, and turned to follow the line of Daphne's pointing finger and observe, rising from his seat, the white-bearded old man, looking somewhat bemused and distressed by being suddenly awake.

'Oh, well, Mr Froggitt is something of an exception, it's true. But—'

'We need *Mrs Beeton's Household Management*,' said Emily Lime. 'And *The Complete History of British Waterways* by N. P. Newell, *Beetles of the World* by G. P. Honeycraft, and the largest book you have on carpentry for beginners. Also we need whatever you have on the history and science of fingerprinting, but *not* just the obvious ones like Herschel.'

Miss Scruton stared down at her. Emily Lime stared back up.

'If you wouldn't mind,' said Daphne.

With a sneer Miss Scruton turned on her heel and sped away.

George gazed after her. 'How is it possible,' he wondered aloud, 'to stomp that angrily but make no sound?'

'How is it possible that she's a member of the Librarians' Guild?' said Emily Lime. 'Utterly inept! Now, you two go and fetch whatever they have on Dutch art of the seventeenth century. I'm off to Criminal Law.'

George and Daphne found their way to the Art section and quickly located the only relevant volume. George opened the book at the index.

'Nothing much on van Biergaarten in here, by the looks of it. Seems as if he really was a bit of a nobody.'

'Well, that's not much use then,' said Daphne. 'Though at least I can understand why we're look-ing. Whereas . . . *Mrs Beeton*?' She gave a confused shrug. 'How on earth is a cookery book going to help us?'

'Who knows?' said George. 'But there's no use arguing with her.'

'She has so much to learn,' said Cordelia Scruton, having seemingly appeared from thin air behind them. George and Daphne nearly leaped out of their skin, though silently of course, because they were in a library.

'*Household Management*,' said Miss Scruton,

laying down a huge leather-bound book on a nearby table. 'Waterways. Beetles. Carpentry.' She placed three more monumental tomes on top of the first. 'And fingerprints.' She added two further slim volumes to the pile. 'Not much, I'm afraid. But I've also marked some passages in these which may be relevant.' She added another three books, each with a bookmark sticking out and attired in gaudy covers. They looked familiar.

'Smeeton Westerby mysteries?' said George, perplexed.

'Yes. I know they're fiction, but I happen to know that the author is meticulous in his research. The procedures described should be accurate enough to prove useful.' Scruton looked from George to Daphne and back again. 'A good librarian is resourceful like that. Speaking of which: have you any news of Mrs Crump?'

'Just a Christmas card,' said George. 'Postmarked Switzerland, funnily enough. I assume she must be in a clinic for her nerves or something. Do you know her, then?'

'Oh, indeed! Margaret and I studied together. There's no finer librarian I've ever met.' Miss Scruton's face softened for a moment, then cemented itself back into a vision of contempt as she stared over the children's heads. 'Anyone with a whit of sense would think twice before trying to fill her shoes.'

George and Daphne followed her gaze to see Emily Lime approaching with more books.

'Thank y— Oh!' Daphne turned back to find that Scruton had departed as silently as she had arrived. 'How *does* she do that?'

'Top-level librarian skills,' said George.

'Tch!' Emily Lime scowled at the books on the table, then raised an eyebrow at the Smeeton

Westerby titles. She picked one up, opened it to the marked page and read. Then she did the same with the other two. The nod she gave then was almost imperceptible.

'Useful?' said George.

'Adequate,' sniffed Emily Lime. 'I suppose.'

They checked out the books and left, only slightly staggering under the weight of them. Daphne gave Cordelia Scruton a smile and an awkward wave as they passed.

'She was quite helpful, really.'

'Yes,' said George. 'Lime just can't stand it if anyone doesn't do things her way.'

'Of course,' said Emily Lime. 'My way is the best. Even if I do need to keep the Holcroft girl around to enforce any kind of order.'

'Oh, *that's* why she's there so much nowadays,' said Daphne.

'Yes,' said Emily Lime. 'She's a useful security measure. But as she isn't library staff, when she threatens girls with extreme violence she's merely *expressing her personality in a spontaneous manner* rather than enforcing outdated and repressive rules.'

George smelled something fishy. And for once it was nothing to do with the contents of his pockets. 'Hang on, though,' he said. 'Just how spontaneous is it? What else is Hulky getting out of the deal, Lime?'

'Well, I may have given her the rest of our supply of sugar mice—'

'*Our* supply? You mean *my* sugar mice!'

'. . . and some help with her reading.'

'You . . . ?!' George ran out of bluster. 'You're giving her reading lessons?'

'Yes. She's utterly hopeless, of course.'

'But you're helping her.' George's face collapsed into a fragile smile. 'Good for you, Emily Lime.'

They walked on in awkward silence for a moment.

'I mean, you're still an utter nutcase, obviously, but . . . Oh, by the way, why *do* we need a copy of *Mrs Beeton* to get to see Mr Thanet?'

'You'll see,' said Emily Lime.

SEVENTEEN

The desk sergeant at Pilkington police station looked up from his crossword and over his counter at the three diminutive figures who had just entered. If he felt any delight at what he saw he did a very good job of hiding it.

'Shouldn't you all be at school?' he said.

Emily Lime adjusted her spectacles to maximize the effect of her hard stare and clumped over to the desk.

'Under ordinary circumstances,' she said, 'we would be.' George and Daphne shuffled up to join her on either side, each swaying slightly under the weight of the piles of books they were carrying. 'But these are not ordinary circumstances.'

'Oh no?' said the sergeant, laying down his ballpoint pen and abandoning all thoughts of six down.

'No,' said Emily Lime, leaning forward to bring her own eyeballs as close as possible to the sergeant's. 'These are *extraordinary* circumstances!'

'Are they now?' The sergeant pulled his head back a little. 'How's that then?'

'You have detained in these premises a client of ours.'

The sergeant gave Emily Lime a quizzical look. 'Bit young to be a lawyer, aren't you?' he said, smiling.

'I'm not a lawyer,' said Emily Lime. 'Nothing so trivial.' She paused for dramatic effect. 'I am . . . a *librarian*!'

'That's as may be, miss, but—'

'And as such, I am entitled under statute 73b, subsection 4 of the Librarians' Code' – Emily Lime slammed the impressive-looking giant book of waterways onto the desk. A cloud of dust rose from its pages obscuring the sergeant's view of its title

– 'to carry out a spot check upon your cells to ensure that all prisoners have been supplied with adequate reading material . . .'

As the dust cloud began to dissipate the sergeant turned his watering eyes to the cover of the book.

'. . . as specified by the 1843 Prisoners' Literature Act.'

Emily Lime slammed down *Mrs Beeton's Household Management* on top of the waterways

book and sent a fresh blast of dust up the sergeant's nose. Keeping one hand over most of the title she prodded the index finger of her other hand at a point just in front of his eyes.

'And amended and updated in Lord Hurley's reform of 1897.'

She thumped *Woodworking: A Needlessly Thorough Introduction* dustily onto the book pile.

'But of course you knew all that.'

'I, um . . . I . . .' said the sergeant, his nose twitching, his eyes crossed as he focused on Emily Lime's finger, and a teardrop trailing down his cheek. 'That is, I . . . I . . . I—' The sergeant raised a hand submissively, stepped backward and turned his face away. 'AATCHOO!'

'Bless you,' said George and Daphne together.

Emily Lime placed an actual law book on the top of the pile. 'So, if you could just show us through to the cells?'

The sergeant blew his nose, cowered slightly before the mighty tower of books, then nodded towards a door. 'You'd best come through,' he said, lifting a hinged section of the counter to join them.

Emily Lime redistributed the books to her beasts of burden and the three of them followed the sergeant through the door.

'Who are—?' began a constable coming the other way.

'Librarians,' said the sergeant.

The constable frowned. 'Are they allowed—?'

'Don't argue with them,' said the sergeant. 'They've got *books*!'

'Your lucky day,' said the sergeant through the small hatch in Mr Thanet's cell door. 'Some more visitors for you.'

'Oh, thank goodness. Is it—' began Mr Thanet, then ground to a halt when the door opened.

Half-risen from his bed, dropping the notebook and pencil he had been holding, he looked from George to Daphne to Emily Lime, and then to the sergeant.

'Really?' he said.

The sergeant shrugged. 'I'll send some tea.'

It wasn't roomy in Mr Thanet's cell. Nor was it cosy. There was a narrow bed with grey blankets, and a bare bulb hanging from the ceiling. A constable brought in a couple of metal-framed chairs after he had delivered a tray of tea in chipped mugs, then left. The metal door clanged shut behind him and they heard the door lock, then receding footsteps.

Mr Thanet sat at one end of the bed, his hands clasped around a mug of tea, and George sat at the other.

'I don't suppose there's a file hidden in any of those?' said Mr Thanet in a forced cheerful tone, pointing at the books piled on the floor. 'You know,' he went on, in a mock whisper, 'so I can escape.'

Emily Lime gave him a pitying look at short range from the nearest of the chairs. 'How on earth could there be?'

'You know: you cut a hole in some of the pages in the middle to make a space for it? I saw it in a film once.'

Emily Lime glared at him. *Cut a hole in some of the pages?*' she said. 'Deliberately damage a library book? Are you quite mad?'

'You really need to learn when people are joking, Lime,' said George.

'Thank you, George.' Mr Thanet gave him a grateful nod.

'As if Mr Thanet would have a clue how to use a file!' George rolled his eyes. 'Anyway, he's innocent so there's no need for escape plans. They're bound to let you go soon, Mr T.'

'I'm not so sure, I'm afraid. I mean, I am innocent, of course. But – it's the oddest thing – they got the painting back in the post this morning.'

'Blimey! That was quick for second class,' muttered George in surprise, then shot an alarmed glance at Mr Thanet to see if he had heard. 'So, er, isn't that good news then? Doesn't that put you in the clear?'

'Well, no. No it doesn't, because apparently my fingerprints are all over the frame.'

'Eh?' said George. '*Your* fingerprints? Ahem. I mean, your *fingerprints*?'

'Yes. And someone else's too. But they're so buttery and smudged, they're proving impossible to identify, apparently.' He shook his head.

'But how did yours get on there?' Daphne asked.

'All I can think is that I must have touched the frame when I almost fell against it at the gallery.'

'That would explain it,' said George.

'But,' said Emily Lime, 'not how it got into your cottage.'

'What?' Mr Thanet looked genuinely shocked.

'It was in a bag under your stairs,' said George. 'I found it when I was looking for a hat. And I took it away because . . . Well, because I know you didn't steal it. Someone else must have put it there to get you into trouble. Any idea who it might be? Anyone got a grudge against you?'

Mr Thanet shook his head.

'Or do you have any idea how the painting could have got there?' said Daphne.

'No. But then any number of the girls could pick my lock, I'm sure. It doesn't even close properly sometimes. I tried to fix it, but— Oh, hang on . . . if it was under the stairs, then . . . I can't tell you *how* the painting got there, but I can at least give you an idea of *when*. I dropped my keys when I was getting my coat to go out to the pub. I had to spend a couple of minutes rummaging through all the rubbish I've got there to find them. I'm sure I would have noticed if the painting was there then. So it must have been put there that night – the night of my birthday – while I was out.'

'That seems reasonable,' said Daphne. 'But wouldn't you have noticed if it was there when you hung your coat up when you got home?'

Mr Thanet looked sheepish. 'No. No, I wouldn't have noticed much at all by then. They had a new beer on at the pub and it turns out it was quite strong, and . . . Well, it's a wonder I made it home at all, to be honest.' He winced at the memory, then fixed Daphne with a serious stare. 'Never go drinking with teachers,' he said.

There was a knock at the door, then the wooden partition slid open and a pair of eyes peered in through the tiny window.

'Right! Out, you lot!' said Inspector Bright as the door swung open. Then: 'Not you, Thanet. Just the children.'

'Oh, but can I just—' Mr Thanet grabbed a

notebook and pencil from under the bed, hurriedly scribbled something on a random page, then tore it out and handed it to Daphne. 'My mother's telephone number. Let her know I'm all right, please?'

Daphne just stared at him.

'You might fool my sergeant with your books, Miss Lime,' said the inspector, motioning George and Emily Lime through the door with one hand while grabbing Daphne by the shoulder with the other. 'But I've stewed enough rabbits in my time to recognize a copy of *Mrs Beeton* when I see one. Go on, hop it!'

He ejected Daphne then turned back to Mr Thanet.

'And if I find out that wasn't really your niece earlier, then there will be extra trouble for you, sir, on top of the generous amount in which you already find yourself.'

And with that he closed the door with an authoritative clunk that echoed through the corridor.

'Well, that was . . . brief,' said George, after the sergeant had enthusiastically ejected them all back onto the street.

They set off back towards the centre of town, their misty breath catching the last of the afternoon's golden light as they went.

'But at least you got to leave that beginner's guide to carpentry for Mr T to read, eh, Lime?'

'He may as well try to improve himself while he's there. And he really does have a *lot* of room for improvement.'

'You don't worry about kicking a man when he's down, do you?'

Emily Lime considered this for a moment as they stopped at the kerb's edge waiting to cross the road. 'Surely that is simply the most practical time to kick a man, isn't it? It's easier, more effective, and less likely to cause strain to the biceps femoris muscle.'

George swallowed back a tide of pointless argument and switched tack. 'The point is: we have to get him out of there as soon as possible.'

'And how are we going to do that? A tunnel?'

'Don't talk daft, Lime. We're going to prove him innocent. Aren't we, Daffers?' He turned to Daphne now and noticed for the first time the downward tilt of her head, and the tightness in her face. 'Daphne?' he said softly.

Daphne blinked and looked his way. 'The thing is . . .' She winced. 'I don't *want* to, but—'

'What?'

'Well, I think he must be guilty.'

'What? Why?'

'His fingerprints are on the frame of the painting.'

'Well, he explained that. He said he fell against it when the runaway train over there' – George pointed at Emily Lime – 'barged into him from behind.'

'No,' said Daphne sadly. 'He said he *must* have fallen against it.' She sighed. 'But I saw the whole thing, and I remember it perfectly. And he *didn't* touch the painting.' She looked straight into George's eyes, tears brimming in her own. 'At least . . . not then.'

'But—' said George. And then he stopped, because he realized he had no more words to follow.

'No.' Emily Lime's voice was as abrasive as ever.

'No?' whimpered George.

'No?' said Daphne. 'You think he did touch the frame?'

'No!' said Emily Lime. 'You say he didn't, and you do have an adequate memory. But it's interesting that he said that.'

'What, exactly?' said Daphne. They had all come to a halt now and naturally drifted into a tight huddle.

'He said he *must* have fallen against the painting. If he wanted to lie to us about it then he'd just say that he had. But he said he *must* have.'

'As if he was trying to make sense of it all himself?' said George.

'I suppose,' said Daphne. 'But that's hardly going to convince a jury, is it?'

'No, of course not,' said Emily Lime. 'Twelve random members of the public? Most of them will be idiots! But it's convinced me.'

'So what do we do now, then?' said George.

Then he walked into the back of Daphne who had come to a sudden halt on the pavement and was gazing, open-mouthed, across the road at the art gallery.

'Daffers! Can't you look where you're . . . well, where *I'm* going?'

Daphne waggled a pointy finger to indicate a figure disappearing through the gallery door.

'What is it?' said George.

'Well, she's dressed rather oddly,' said Daphne. 'But I'm sure that was Molly Fox!'

EIGHTEEN

George reached for the gallery door but his fingertips stopped inches short. Then he was wrenched backwards by a sharp jerk on his coat collar. He turned grumpily to Emily Lime and Daphne, each of whom was now wiping her hands.

'I wish you didn't feel quite so free to push and pull me around.'

'I wish I *never* had to touch you at all,' said Emily Lime, working away vigorously with a dampened handkerchief at the stubborn black smudge on her palm. 'But sometimes you leave me no choice.'

'It's just that, after the last time we were here,' said Daphne, adopting a gentler tone, 'we can't exactly expect a warm welcome.'

'Ah! Good point.'

They stepped away from the door. Daphne and Emily Lime sat on the steps while George paced about.

'But Molly Fox is in there! And it was her pencil in Mr T's cottage!'

'Well, maybe,' said Daphne. 'We don't know for—'

'They *might* not recognize us as St Rita's pupils,' said George. 'If we keep our coats buttoned up to hide our uniform.'

'They'll still know we ought to be at school,' said Emily Lime, 'even if they don't know which one. This Fox girl may be tall enough to get away with it, but we're not.'

'Then what do we do?' said George.

'I think,' said Daphne, 'I may have an idea.'

She pointed at a shiny new coach that had just drawn up at the bottom of the steps. George watched as the door opened and a plump man in a smart overcoat stepped off then stood to one side. A platoon of schoolboys filed out and assembled into neat rows on the wide stone steps. They moved with the military precision of a Roman cohort; their uniforms were uniformly spick and span, and seemed to emanate a glow of almost supernatural cleanliness.

'St Godfrey's!' whispered George, grinning. 'Perfect.'

The plump man climbed the steps to address the regiment of boys. He stood very erect and spoke in a loud, clear voice. 'Now, boys, you will remain here while Mr Craigmuir parks the coach and I step inside for a word with Mr Montague. We are' – he consulted an old-fashioned pocket watch on a chain – 'precisely twelve and a half minutes early. I shall return in eleven and a half minutes time and then you will enter the museum. In the meantime you will silently conjugate Latin verbs in preparation for the test on Thursday.'

He set off up the steps and entered the museum. As soon as he had disappeared through the door, all discipline evaporated. Shoulders slumped, the rigid lines of the boys' military formation softened and a low buzz of chatter started up. George positioned himself a few steps up from them all, hooked the little finger of each hand into the corners of his mouth, and gave an impressive piercing whistle. The junior Roman army rewarded him with their attention.

'Right then,' said George. 'Who doesn't like art, but does like cream buns?'

Ten minutes later, Daphne was pulling a St Godfrey's cap down tightly onto her head and tucking her hair out of sight. 'I thought you said that the library has no money left?' she whispered.

'I said we had no money left for *books*,' whispered

George behind his hand. He adjusted his own cap for the umpteenth time but felt no more comfortable with the result. This was, he reluctantly accepted, only to be expected. His hair was a creature of wild splendour and could not be easily constrained. 'The library's financial systems are deliberately complicated and extremely boring. It's the only way to keep Lime's nose out of them. The catering piggy bank has to be kept entirely separate from the books piggy bank – and secret from Lime – for accounting reasons.'

'And so you can bribe schoolboys with cream buns to lend us their uniforms?'

'That too.'

'This is ridiculous!' said Emily Lime, looking even less happy in her cap than George was in his.

'No,' said George. 'This is a vital and highly sophisticated undercover investigation.' He looked Emily Lime up and down in her borrowed cap, blazer and shorts. 'You, on the other hand, really do look ridiculous. Now, Lime: head down and get in line. Eleven and a half minutes is nearly up and Colonel Grumpy will be back any second. Try to look like a posh boy.'

'She's got a better chance than you,' whispered Daphne.

The teacher appeared at the top of the steps, and descended partway towards the boys whose ranks had reformed into perfect straight lines moments earlier. He cast a critical glance over them, but George, Daphne and Emily Lime, positioned behind three of the tallest boys, remained hidden. George, moving only his eyes, glanced around him. He wasn't used to being amongst other boys and wondered if he ought to feel more at home. But these boys looked more like soldiers: standing to attention, obeying orders, fearful of being disciplined. *Not for me*, he thought.

'I suppose you will do,' pronounced the teacher.

'Now, obviously, during your time in the gallery your behaviour will be impeccable at all times. You will observe the artworks in appreciative silence, taking brief, neat notes to be written up in full later. You may work your way through the gallery by your own routes, but rooms three, eight and thirteen may be used only to access other areas of the gallery. *You will not linger!* They contain *unsuitable sculptures* likely to instil *unseemly thoughts*. Similarly, the east wing is out of bounds completely as it contains only *modern works* produced by degenerates, charlatans and Americans. Do not stray, boys! I will know. And you will not care for the consequences.'

He consulted his watch with an efficient glance.

'You have two hours, then Mr Craigmuir will take us on to the superior enrichment of the Military Museum. No one will delay our departure at fourteen hundred hours precisely. This is, I know, understood by you all. Begin.'

The perfect square of schoolboys marched in step up the stairs, with George, Daphne and Emily Lime imperfectly doing their best to fit in near the centre. George resisted the urge to salute as they passed the teacher, and concentrated on not tripping over.

The square halted at the top of the steps, then each row in turn peeled off to pass through the entrance in single file.

As George followed Daphne into the entrance hall some of the St Godfrey's boys broke into a joyful run. A tall lad passing him noted George's astonishment.

'It's all right. We can pretty much run riot for an hour. Old Gladwin is ex-military, you see. Chap like that likes order and routine, which makes him wonderfully predictable. He'll be having lunch in the Prince George Tavern – steak and kidney pudding and a pint of ale, then a half pint and a pipe for afters – then back to check up on us at *thirteen hundred hours precisely*.'

'When you'll all be behaving yourselves perfectly and taking careful notes, I s'pose?'

'That's about the size of it. Notes in Morse code if we really want to suck up to the old buzzard. Have fun, chummy. But don't get caught. It'd be bad for us all if you did.'

'Up for a court martial?'

'Oh no. No trial. Just beatings all round.'

And with a wave and a smile the tall boy headed

off, to linger amongst the unsuitable sculptures in rooms three, eight and thirteen.

'What now?' said Daphne. 'Should we split up to look for Molly Fox?'

'Of course not!' Emily Lime hitched up her borrowed shorts. 'It's quite obvious where she'll be.' She stomped off.

'Of course not,' said Daphne to George with a shrug, setting off after her.

'Obvious,' said George.

The thing about Emily Lime was, she was really annoying, but she was also very often right. Molly Fox was in the Dutch room, standing in front of a large portrait of a fat Dutch merchant but with her head turned towards the much smaller work immediately to its left, *The Fish Seller's Canary*, Oil on canvas, 1670, by Jan van Biergaarten, 1649–1720. Eight and a quarter inches by eleven and seven eighths. On loan from the collection of Lord and Lady Chorley.

'Well, well.' George scanned the room and noted that today's attendant was one of the gallery's younger, fitter employees. There was also an ancient couple craning their necks to look at *The Fish Seller's Canary*.

'What do you think she's up to?' Daphne whispered.

'I dunno. Maybe if it was her that stole the painting the last time then she's planning to do it again.'

'Well, that's hardly likely, is it?' Emily Lime sneered.

'No. No, it's not,' said George. 'But then if you'd asked me if you were likely to be dressed as a twelve-year-old boy today I'd have said that was unlikely too. So you never know, do you?'

'I'm going to take a closer look,' said Daphne.

She walked over to the side of the old couple so that they screened her from Molly Fox. George glanced over at the attendant, who had risen from his chair now and stretched as if just out of bed. The old couple shuffled in for a closer look at the *Canary*. Daphne scratched an imaginary itch so that her hand shielded her face from Molly. The attendant strolled over with unconvincing casualness.

'I don't like the look of this,' George murmured.

'What did you expect?' sighed Emily Lime.

'Oh, I've given up expecting,' muttered George,

shuffling off towards the painting. 'No good ever comes of it.'

The old couple were now as close to the *Canary* as the low wire barrier would allow and leaning in so far that it looked like they were trying to smell the paint. Molly turned her head, distracted by the still-scratching Daphne in her ill-fitting boy's uniform. A glimmer of recognition had just registered on her face when the attendant stepped between them.

'Excuse me,' he said, addressing the backs of the old couple. 'Excuse me, sir? Madam?' he said again, more loudly but still without provoking a response. 'HEY!' he shouted, at last.

The old woman and her husband, still hunched over, swivelled to face him.

'Eh?' said the old man, staring up through bottle-end spectacles.

'What was that?' said his wife, squinting through her own thick glasses.

'I wonder . . .' began the attendant, then realized his mistake. 'I WONDER,' he continued, 'IF YOU COULD TAKE A STEP AWAY FROM THE PAINTING.'

'Painting?' said the man.

'YES!'

The old couple shuffled on the spot, turning back to face *The Fish Seller's Canary* for a moment. Then the old man leaned in as if to whisper gently into his wife's ear.

'WE'VE GONE WRONG!' he bellowed.

'HOW'S THAT, DEAR?' she shouted back.

'WE'RE IN THE ART GALLERY!'

'OH DEAR.'

The old woman looked around to her right, and then to her left. It took for ever, and then a bit longer. 'I *THOUGHT* IT LOOKED BIG FOR A FISHMONGER'S,' she yelled.

They shuffled round to face the attendant again, each giving a little smile and a shrug, then they moved very, very slowly towards the exit.

The gallery attendant watched them go and shook his head, and so discovered Molly Fox and Daphne either side of him.

'Erm, excuse me, miss . . . ?' he said.

'Yes?' said Molly Fox.

And so did Daphne.

Molly Fox and the attendant both gave her a puzzled look.

'Miss?' said the attendant.

'Oh, *miss*!' said Daphne, in as low a voice as she could manage. 'Thought you said *mister*. Do excuse me, my hearing's a bit shaky at the moment. I, um . . . I've got mud in my ears. From playing . . . rugbyball?'

The attendant dropped his gaze from Daphne's face to examine her ill-fitting uniform: the too-long trouser legs pooling at her shoes; her fingers just peeking out of the sleeves of the blazer; and then his eyes settled on her blazer pocket as a puzzled look formed on his face. 'Oh!' he said at last, pointing at Daphne's blazer badge and smiling. 'You're at St Godfrey's?'

'Um, yes. Yes, I am.'

'I say! How is the old place?'

'Oh, er . . . much the same, you know.'

'Ha! Yes. Wonderful. And is old Heacham still there?'

'Oh, yes. Old Heacham. Yes, indeed. Still . . . there . . .'

'Good Lord! Really? And he must have been eighty back in my day. Extraordinary!'

'Oh, yes. Still going strong.' Daphne looked to George who pulled a face and shrugged in reply.

'He's out of the wheelchair, then?' The attendant looked astonished.

'Um, no. But he's still going strong *in* his wheelchair. Speedy.'

By the look on the attendant's face, this did not seem likely. But then Molly Fox shrieked, which hijacked his attention. George noted Emily Lime scuttling away and pocketing what he suspected was a pair of compasses. Molly Fox rubbed a hand on her left buttock and found herself staring straight into the attendant's eyes.

'Please keep your voice down, miss,' he said. 'It's only natural to be excited by some of our exhibits, but you really . . .' A glimmer of recognition fluttered into his eyes. 'Hang on. Don't I know you?'

'Eh? No, I—'

'Yes! You were here last week. You're from St Rita's!'

'No.'

'Don't deny it. I have an excellent memory for faces.' He turned to Daphne, staring intently into her eyes. 'I wouldn't forget any of that lot. You wouldn't believe how badly they behave at those inferior schools!'

'I can't imagine,' said Daphne.

The attendant turned back to Molly Fox. 'Are you back for another try?'

Molly Fox looked shocked. Her eyes flicked to Daphne. 'But—' she began.

'I think you had better come with me.' The attendant reached out to take hold of Molly's arm, but she pulled away. 'Now, young lady . . .'

But Molly Fox was already three paces away, turning a walk into a run and speeding towards the exit.

'Hey!' The attendant set off after her, leaving George, Daphne and Emily Lime alone in front of *The Fish Seller's Canary*.

'Blimey!' said George, pointing a thumb at the painting. 'If *we* wanted to nick it, now would be the time.'

Daphne was still staring after Molly Fox and the attendant. 'I don't suppose you got a good look at the soles of her shoes, did you?'

'Afraid not, Daffers.' George leaned in for a close look at the painting. 'I see they've fixed this to the wall a lot more securely this time,' he said. 'Definitely beyond Mr T's capabilities now.'

Daphne looked. 'Oh yes! I suppose that's why they've changed the frame too.'

'More likely it's police evidence now,' said Emily Lime. 'With Thanet's fingerprints on it.'

George sighed. He straightened up and considered the painting itself for the first time. 'It's a lot of fuss, all this, for a little yellow bird, isn't it? I mean, it's nice enough but it's hardly the *Mona Lisa*.'

'It *is* curious,' agreed Emily Lime. 'If Mr Thanet stole it, then it was a stupid choice. There are lots of things here that would be easier to take and far more valuable.'

'But if it was stolen just to get Mr Thanet into trouble, then that's even more stupid,' said Daphne.

'Well, *I* can't make any sense of it,' said George. 'We'll just have to catch the real thief and get *them* to explain.' He looked down at his clothes. 'But we'd better swap our uniforms back with those fellas in the café first.'

They started towards the exit.

'And maybe have a bun or two ourselves while we're there.'

'**Y**ou've got jam on your uniform, Lime,' said George as they walked along the corridor towards the library.

'*I* didn't get jam on my uniform,' moaned Emily Lime. 'That wretched boy Nigel did.'

'I think all Nigels must be horrible,' said Daphne. 'My cousin Nigel is just *disgusting*! But at least your Nigel had the decency to look ridiculous in your uniform. That boy Rajiv looked better in my pinafore than I do!'

'It did rather suit him,' said George thoughtfully,

as they arrived outside the library door. 'He wasn't exactly keen to give it back either, was he?' He turned the door handle and pushed the door open with its customary creak. Entering, they were surprised to find that Hulky, in whose capable and meaty hands they had left the library's care, was nowhere to be seen. They were more surprised, though, to find that Molly Fox *was* there, and advancing towards them with furious determination.

'There you are!' she said. 'What the hell have you done with it?'

'What have we done with *what*?' said Daphne.

'What are you talking about?' said George.

'And why must you talk about it *so loudly* in my library?' said Emily Lime.

The three of them started down the steps with Emily Lime in the lead. Molly Fox blocked their path at the bottom like a solid wall of fury. Emily Lime came to a halt on the second to last step, which put the two of them face to face.

'I know what you've done!' Molly Fox jabbed at the air between them with a vicious finger. 'I haven't worked out *how* you did it yet, but the police can deal with that.' Her voice was a snarl. 'But what

I really don't understand is *why*.'

Emily Lime spoke in a calm, quiet voice. 'I have no idea what you're talking about, but if you insist upon continuing to spout this utter drivel then can you at least do it quietly?'

'Oh yes, you'd like me to stay quiet, wouldn't you?'

'Yes! I just said so, didn't I?'

'You and your thieving friends!'

'Look, Molly,' said Daphne, in her most reasonable voice, 'I really think—'

'What's he ever done to you, eh?' Molly Fox stopped jabbing at the air with her finger and began instead to jab it hard into Emily Lime's ribs.

George was confused. He wasn't fond of shouting, or anger, or any kind of fuss really. That's why he'd always liked libraries. They were usually – outside of St Rita's, at least – good places to go for a bit of peace and quiet. But now Hulky had emerged from the office and was clumping over to join the fray, which he thought was unlikely to improve matters.

'Wasn't nearly breaking his neck enough for you?' Molly Fox dug her finger into Emily Lime's side again. 'Eh?'

'Ssh!' said Hulky.

'So you had to get him locked up?' Molly Fox started in on Emily Lime's other side, jabbing away. 'Stuck in that horrible little cell!'

'Oh, so *you* were his other visitor!' muttered Daphne. 'You're not really his niece, are you?'

'What?' Molly Fox gave her a scornful glare. 'No, of course not.' She gave Daphne a jab now. 'And don't try to distract me. It won't work.'

'Ssh!' said Hulky, leaning in close to Molly Fox's ear.

'And don't try to shut me up! I won't be silenced! That poor man! That gentle, generous, sensitive man!'

'Um, how do you mean?' said George.

'He's been teaching me to *draw*! Why? What did you think I meant?'

'Nothing,' said George hurriedly. 'Drawing lessons, you say?'

'Yes, he was teaching me at his cottage. He's very talented, actually, unlike that idiot Deakins. Giving up his time out of the kindness of his heart. But YOU . . . you lot go ruining his life just for . . . what? For your AMUSEMENT?' Her voice was a hysterical shriek now, her face a livid portrait of rage.

'*Please* be quiet,' said Hulky in a whispered rumble.

'What kind of MONSTERS are you?' yelled Molly Fox.

'Ssh!' said Hulky.

'We are not *monsters*!' Emily Lime's voice was an angry, tremulous whisper. 'We are *librarians*!'

'YOU—' shouted Molly Fox, with another vicious jab of her finger.

And that's when Hulky hit her.

'You really shouldn't have done that,' said Emily Lime, kneeling beside Molly Fox lying unconscious in a pile of books at the bottom of History and Geography. 'We'll have to reshelve these now.'

George lifted *A History of Polynesia* from Molly Fox's face and examined the damage.

'She's out cold, but she's breathing,' he said.

'I should hope so,' said Emily Lime. 'Death in the library is strictly forbidden.'

'What should we do with her?' said Daphne. 'We can't take her to Matron.'

'No,' said George. 'We need her alive.' He thought for a moment. 'Let's bung her in the office for now.'

Daphne considered this. 'All right. You take her arms and I'll take her legs.'

Grunting with effort they lifted Molly Fox, took two paces, then dropped her to the floor again with an indelicate thump.

'Shh!' said Emily Lime.

'*Or* we could both take her arms and drag her,' said George.

'Good idea.'

They dragged her slowly across the library

floor and in through the office door. It was a bit of a struggle, but they managed it eventually, and the door only closed on Molly's head a couple of times. They cleared the top of Emily Lime's desk and, at the third attempt, managed to lift Molly onto it. George folded his coat and tucked it under her head as a pillow, then leaned against the desk struggling to get his breath back. Daphne rearranged Molly's pinafore and limbs, finding in the process that one of her shoes had come off.

'Oh!'

She scanned the floor and eventually spotted the missing shoe peeking out from behind a pile of books just inside the doorway. She went over and picked it up.

'Oh!' she said again.

'What . . . is it?' gasped George.

'It *was* the left one we needed to see, wasn't it?' Daphne held up the shoe. 'No crack in the sole.'

George shrugged. 'No,' he said. 'She wasn't exactly acting guilty, was she? That would have been a pretty amazing bluff.'

'But why was she accusing *us*.' Daphne thought for a moment. 'And of what, for that matter?' She

thought back. '*What the hell have you done with it?*' she muttered.

'Eh?'

'When we first came in, she said, *What the hell have you done with it?* With what?'

'Dunno. She wasn't making much sense at all if you ask me.' He looked at Molly lying peacefully on the desk as Daphne removed the other shoe and placed the pair on the floor. He shook his head. 'Arty crafty types,' he said. 'I'll never understand them.'

'But she was so defensive of Mr Thanet, she can't have set him up to be arrested, can she?' Daphne moved to the door and opened it.

'If he *has* been giving her drawing lessons then I suppose that explains her pencil being in his cottage,' mused George. 'But we only have her word for that.'

They left the office and George locked the door behind him.

'You think they're' – Daphne hesitated – '*romantically involved*?'

'Blimey!' said George. 'No! I don't think— I mean, Mr Thanet is ancient, isn't he? He must be thirty, I reckon! Or nearly thirty anyway.' He pondered this some more as they made their way back to Emily Lime and Hulky. 'You don't really think . . . ?'

'I don't know. She denied it almost too much, I thought.'

George squirmed briefly. 'I don't even want to think about it,' he said. 'And either way, it doesn't help us work out who stole the painting.' He frowned. 'Or why, for that matter. Oi, Lime!' He tapped Emily Lime on the shoulder and she turned to face him, showing no great sense of delight. 'Did you say that the painting gets a mention in one of our books?'

'Yes,' said Emily Lime. 'Gertrude Planck writes

about *The Fish Seller's Canary* in passing in *Dutch Masters of the 17th Century*, and the artist who painted it, van Biergaarten, has a brief entry in the *Dictionary of Artists.*'

'Anything that would explain why someone would steal it?'

'No. It's a minor work by a very minor artist.'

'At least according to Gertrude Planck,' said Daphne. 'Whoever she is.'

'She's an *expert.*' Emily Lime sounded affronted. 'She wrote a book!'

'Hang on,' said George. 'Daffers has a point. Just because this woman Planck doesn't rate van what's-his-name, doesn't mean to say there won't be other *experts* who disagree. This is the whole problem with arty craftiness: nobody can ever decide once and for all what's what. There's no proper rules.'

'What does it say in the book from the town library?' said Daphne.

'Nothing,' said Emily Lime. 'Really we need—'

The door creaked open. 'Hello, library folk!'

They turned to see Miss Deakins the art mistress at the top of the stairs.

'Yes?' said Emily Lime, with casual rudeness.

'You haven't seen Molly Fox, have you? Lower sixth girl? About this high, ruddy-faced, hair like a bird's nest?'

George gave Hulky a significant look to silence her.

'She's not here, I'm afraid,' said Daphne, which George noted was sort of true. 'Why do you ask?'

'We're trying to find her, and someone said they thought they'd seen her heading this way.'

'Well, as you can see . . .' Daphne raised her arms to indicate the emptiness of the room.

'Hey ho.' Miss Deakins looked not at all disappointed. 'Probably just as well. I'm afraid it's the police who want a word with her. Apparently she was seen in the gallery today, hanging about near that *Canary* painting. You wouldn't have any idea why she might go there, would you?'

'No, miss,' said Daphne, while the others shook their heads.

'No, of course not.' Miss Deakins turned to go.

'Oh, miss?' George said.

Miss Deakins turned back. 'Yes? George, isn't it?'

'Yes, miss. I was wondering – well, we all were . . . We were just talking about that painting as it happens.'

'Oh yes?'

'Yuss. And, well, we're all a bit shocked and upset about Mr Thanet.'

'Yes, it must be hard for you. You must feel . . . let down. Betrayed, even.'

'Oh yuss, miss. Very let down. And we just . . . well, we can't understand why he did it, really. We heard it's not even worth all that much. Would you know anything about that, with being an art mistress and all?'

Miss Deakins gave a sad little shake of her head. 'I'm afraid it's really not my area, all that drab *realistic* painting. It had its place in its day, I suppose. But, really, it's of no interest now. Not when there's Pollock, Rothko, Dubuffet . . . Ah! The colours! The energy! The life!' She stopped to take a breath, then her face fell. 'But I suppose such *challenging* art may not be for everyone. And a pretty painting of a little bird might appeal to some people's . . . less sophisticated tastes.' She raised her eyebrows, as if a thought had just occurred to her. 'In fact, it's not so unlike the sort of pictures your Mr Thanet likes. He was telling me about the ones in his cottage when we were celebrating his birthday at the pub.' She looked away into space. 'How odd to think of us celebrating so innocently with him only days ago . . .'

She touched a hand to her face, then remained quite still for a long moment.

'Oh, but forgive me, children. I fear I've been of precious little help to you. And now, I really must get on and try to find the elusive Miss Fox. Perhaps I shall try the sanatorium next. After those girls got so sick before the trip I've been worried that there might be some kind of bug going around.' She looked at them, concern furrowing her brow. '*You're* not feeling poorly, are you?' she said.

'No, miss. Right as rain, aren't we?' said George.

Daphne and Emily Lime mumbled, 'Yes, miss,' while Hulky gave a low grunt of agreement.

'That's a relief at least,' said Miss Deakins. 'Well, ta-ta for now. And if you do see this Fox girl, send her my way so we can get this whole police business cleared up.'

'We'll let her know you're looking for her,' said Daphne. 'If we see her.'

'Jolly good.' Miss Deakins looked at them all one last time. 'You poor dears,' she said, and then, with a creak of the door, she was gone.

'Well, she wasn't much use,' said George.

'Except . . .' Daphne gave her chin a thoughtful massage. 'Like Mr Thanet said: the painting must have been put in his cottage while he was in the pub.'

'Well, yuss,' said George. 'So . . . ?'

'So,' said Emily Lime, 'logically, whoever was with him wasn't placing stolen art in his home.'

'So if we find out who was there,' said Daphne, 'well, it won't tell us who did it, but it should at least rule a few people out. But who do we ask about that? Miss Deakins? If she was there then I suppose we can rule her out as a suspect. But do we want her to know that we're investigating?'

'No, I don't trust her,' said George. 'Arty crafty type.'

'So what do we do?' said Daphne.

George gave her a pitying look. 'Isn't it obvious?' he said. 'We go to the pub.'

'We can't go to the pub!' said Daphne.

George had expected this. 'I know what you're thinking: it's a long way and we're all tired from traipsing round Pilkington, and it'll be dark. But it's OK, we can borrow bicycles and lamps.'

'I don't think,' said Emily Lime, 'that it's *how* we get there that's worrying Deirdre.'

'Daphne,' said Daphne wearily.

'As I was saying: I don't think it's our means of transport that worries *Daphne*, more the matter of three children under the age of sixteen entering premises used exclusively or primarily for the sale of alcohol, as specifically forbidden by the Licensing Act of 1902.'

'Oh,' said George. 'That. Yes.'

'Actually,' said Daphne, 'no.'

She drank in their surprise for a moment before continuing.

'I would imagine that in a village like Pelham the policing of the village pub will be lax at best, and the landlord will only be glad of some extra trade. No, the reason I said we can't go is: we've no money. Unless you have another secret piggy bank for drinks?'

'No. And we can't borrow from the cream bun money either because that's all gone.'

'Well, then,' said Daphne, 'I think we can probably get the landlord to turn a blind eye to us if we at least have a lemonade each. But not if we don't buy anything at all.'

'You're right,' said George. 'What we need is a short-term loan. But not from Lilian Coleby in the first form, obviously. Her interest rates are diabolical.' He contemplated the matter for a moment. 'Let's have a look in Molly Fox's pockets.' He started towards the library office door.

'George!' Daphne looked appalled. 'You can't steal money from an unconscious girl.'

'Well, I'm not stealing it from a conscious one. That's always gone *very* badly in the past. And we're not stealing, we're borrowing. We'll pay her back. Somehow. Eventually.'

He unlocked the door and led them all into the office.

The desk was empty, and a cold breeze blew in through the open window.

'Oh, heck!' said George. 'She's legged it! That is very inconsiderate.'

They stood there in silence for a moment. Hulky frowned down at her fist, as if rebuking it for a job poorly done.

'But I don't think she'll go to the police,' said George. 'So it shouldn't matter too much that she's got away.'

'Just the same,' said Daphne, 'we should get a move on. If we're going to a pub then we need money. So let's ask someone with lots of it.'

George looked at her. 'Marion?' he said.

'Marion,' she said.

'That,' said George, 'is a very good idea.'

'You don't mind, do you?' said Marion.

Emily Lime made an unhappy noise.

'No,' said Daphne, sounding as if she very much did. 'Not at all.'

She glanced behind her as they cycled along. A dozen or so bicycle lamps danced like fireflies, trailing behind her in the deep dark of the winter's night. 'It's just that . . . well, we were already a bit worried about being discreet, and quiet, and trying not to draw attention to ourselves . . .'

'I quite understand, old thing, I really do. Only, obviously I had to ask Cicely along. Can't go anywhere without my best chum Cicely now, can I? And then, well, the rest of the fifth form heard we were going and *they* all wanted to come too. I had to fight pretty hard to keep the numbers down to two per bicycle.'

Daphne sighed and leaned hard on the pedals as the road rose in a gentle incline towards the Ploughman's Rest public house. It was a modest building, set on a rise on the approach to Pelham village, a dark soft shape against the deep blue night, with just two tall narrow windows visible, glimmering with warm light, suggesting life within.

'Besides, I've made it very clear that it's soft drinks only, everyone on their best behaviour, and home to bed by nine thirty, so it'll just be a jolly little outing and no trouble at all.'

'Yes,' said Daphne, fully aware that the *best behaviour* of many of the fifth formers was border-line criminal.

Behind her, George gave a low groan, but whether this was because he was thinking the same thing, or because of the exercise, Daphne could not be sure, and before she could ask, they had arrived.

The girls drew to a halt in an excited gaggle and deposited a tangle of bicycles along the rear wall. Then Marion, accompanied by Cicely, led them inside. George and Emily Lime followed Daphne in, cringing at the sound of the Fives behind them, fizzing like a shaken-up bottle of pop, ready to explode.

'Hey ho, landlord!' cried Marion, waving energetically to a stocky man behind the bar and gaining the attention of absolutely everyone in the place.

'*Discreet and quiet*,' muttered George, and rolled his eyes at Daphne.

'Now see here, miss . . .' The landlord leaned

forward, braced against the bar, his eyes narrowed.

Marion beamed at him and produced a ten-pound note from her coat pocket. 'Sixteen glasses of lemonade, two ginger beers and a bottle of Château Lafite '28, please, barkeep,' she said.

The landlord rubbed his chin, eyed the tenner, considered for a second, then smiled. 'I'm afraid we're right out of Lafite '28, miss. Old Frank there had the last bottle just yesterday as it goes. Ain't that right, Frank?' He looked over to a ragged old fellow by the fire nursing a half pint of murky stout.

'Oh, ar,' said Frank.

'Yes, old Frank is a right devil for his vintage Bordeaux. We can't hardly keep the stuff in the place he gets through it so fast. So will it be *seven*-teen lemonades and two ginger beers, p'raps?'

'Do you know, that would be just splendid,' said Marion. 'Oh, and could you rustle us up some grub too, maybe?'

'I daresay I could make you up a plate or two of sandwiches, that you and your friends could eat in the back room, where you might be more comfortable.' He pointed to a door. 'So as the chief constable over there doesn't disturb you all if his game of dominoes gets a bit heated, like.'

'Oh, I quite understand,' said Marion. 'That's just marvellous. Thanks ever so.' She took a look over at the game of dominoes in question and gave the chief constable a friendly wave. 'Evening, Uncle Donald,' she said, then addressing the fifth formers: 'Saloon bar for us lot, girls. Move on through. Grub and fizzy pop for all. And remember: no fighting until we're back outside.'

The fifth formers did as they were told and jostled through to the back room. Marion settled up with the landlord, including payment for two pints of beer sent over to Uncle Donald and his opponent, and then followed on. George, Daphne and Emily Lime collected the three glasses that Marion had left for them on the bar.

George balanced himself on the footrail so that he could lean an elbow on the bar and whisper to the landlord, 'You, er, weren't working the other night when a bunch of St Rita's staff came in, were you? It was a birthday celebration, and—'

The landlord hushed him with a finger to his lips. He glanced to each side, as if checking whether they might be overheard, then he leaned in close to

George's ear. 'Get in the back room, or you'll feel my boot. OK?' Then he gave George the unfriendliest smile that he had ever seen.

'Right you are,' said George.

As they were on their way, they heard the front door open, and the landlord's cheerful welcome to a new arrival. George jerked down below the level of the bar and signalled Emily Lime and Daphne to do likewise. From this position, just outside the door to the saloon and to one side of the bar, they were hidden, for now at least, from the landlord and the drinkers on the other. Here, the only customer was hidden behind a newspaper, leaving the children entirely unobserved.

'How does this help us, exactly?' said Emily Lime.

'Well, we won't get very far just drinkin' lemonade with the bloomin' fifth form, will we?' hissed George.

'No,' said Emily Lime. 'Obviously our time will be much better spent on our hands and knees on the carpet.'

'On the really disturbingly *sticky* floor,' said Daphne, examining the palm of one hand and frowning.

'Yes,' said Emily Lime. 'It's disgusting. And it's

smokier here than in the sixth form common room.'

There was indeed a considerable fug, despite there being so few customers.

'Hmm . . .' George turned his attention back to the figure hidden behind the newspaper and realized that here was the source of most of the smoke. He sniffed the air. 'Capstan full strength,' he said. 'And I can't be sure through all the smoke' – he pointed to the newspaper – 'but I think that's a copy of the *Racing Post*.'

'Oh yes!' said Daphne. 'I recognize those gnarled hands.'

'I smell a nun,' said George. 'Come on!'

They cast a glance to the landlord, pulling a pint of stout for the newcomer, then scuttled over, swinging round and rising in a tight huddle behind the newspaper reader's chair.

'Hello, Sister,' whispered George.

'Strike a light, Georgie Boy,' said Sister Adelaide, St Rita's Divinity and Philosophy mistress, without looking round. 'Can't an honest nun even get a bit of peace and quiet in her local boozer these days, then? What're you doing here?' She turned her head just a fraction, cocking an ear to him.

'Oh, you know, a little pushbike outing. A healthy body and a healthy mind, and all that gubbins. Stopped off for refreshments before we head back.'

'Ha!' Sister Adelaide released a fresh (though also not at all fresh) cloud of smoke out over the top of her paper. 'You're about as keen on exercise as I am on Butcher's Boy in the two-thirty at Haydock tomorrow.'

'Um . . . ?'

'Gah! Don't they teach you anything at . . . Scratch that. 'Course I know they don't. *You*, Georgie Boy, do not take bike rides for the good of your health. They're more likely to finish you off than make you fitter, the state you're in. Wotcha really 'ere for, boy?'

'Well, we were hoping to talk to the landlord, but he's not exactly keen, so maybe you could give us a hand?'

''Appy to 'elp if I can, Georgie Boy. I know you'll see me right, eh?'

'Course, Sister. So, er, do you come here often?'

'Oh yes, Georgie. I'm a regular worshipper.' She raised her glass of stout, white-topped and black-bodied like her nun's habit, only cleaner.

'So were you here for Mr Thanet's birthday?' said Daphne, rather too eagerly.

'Oh, so that's it, is it? You playing detectives again, are you?'

'Maybe,' said George coyly. 'So *were* you here?'

'Might've been, Georgie Boy. Might very well 'ave. But I 'eard Thanet was bang to rights. Is that wrong?'

'We're wondering if someone else could have done it,' said Daphne, 'and Mr Thanet has just been, um . . . *fitted in*?'

'Ha! Fitted *up*, girly.' Sister Adelaide turned the

page of her *Racing Post* and thought for a moment. 'Could well be,' she said at last. 'I wouldn't say Thanet *wouldn't* do it, mind. Lord knows, anyone can take a wrong turn if circumstances dictate. But I reckon 'e *couldn't*. And stealing art's a mug's game at the best of times. Ain't necessarily that 'ard to nick it, but it's a nightmare to shift once you do. Not worth the bother, unless you get something *really* tasty, *and* you 'ave a buyer lined up in advance. Nah, I reckon you're right. 'E's been framed for it. What was it, anonymous tip-off?'

'Yuss,' said George.

'Yurr.' Sister Adelaide lit a new cigarette from the butt of the old one, drew in a deep, corrosive breath and gave a resonant cough. 'Always a bit iffy, your anonymous phone call. So what's Thanet's birthday got to do with it?'

'We think the stolen painting was planted in his cottage while he was here that night,' said Daphne. 'So if we knew who else was here ... ?'

'Hmm . . . well, lessee . . . I *was* 'ere, as it goes, but not with that lot. They was in the saloon. I kept myself to myself over 'ere. Don't think any of 'em even noticed me, apart from Thanet. 'E gave me a nod and offered to buy me a pint on 'is way through. Got 'ere about, ooh . . . quarter past eight. That Miss Deakins was already 'ere, Quirk and Fotheringay too. And Miss Cosgrove, I reckon. At least I 'eard 'er motorbike. And Woolley, but she was a bit later. Oh, and she left early too. As far as I could make out she weren't feeling right so Deakins phoned a taxi and took 'er back to school.'

'Oh, yuss?' said George. 'And was this a while before Mr Thanet left?'

'Yurr. An hour or more, I reckon. And when Thanet went 'ome 'e was a bit the worse for wear so 'e might not 'ave been too speedy getting back neither.'

'Interesting.'

'Cosgrove and Quirk was last to leave, maybe ten minutes later.'

'But Cosgrove would have overtaken Mr Thanet on her motorbike?' said Daphne.

'Obviously!' said Emily Lime. 'A Triumph Thunderbird 6T (with a 650cc engine generating 34 horse power) has a top speed of over 100 m.p.h.'

Sister Adelaide looked round and raised a quizzical eyebrow. 'Well, well, Library Girl? You got a secret life as a Speedway star or summink?'

'No. Don't be ridiculous!' said Emily Lime. 'But I ordered in a new manual for Miss Cosgrove after she spilled oil on the last one, so obviously I read it before I passed it on to her.' Then, when this proved insufficient to remove the looks of surprise from the faces of the others, she added: 'It was only short,' as if this would explain everything.

'So any one of Miss Woolley, Miss Deakins and Miss Cosgrove,' said Daphne, abandoning all talk of motorcycles, 'could have got to Mr Thanet's cottage before he got home.'

'Or any girl in the school, of course,' said Sister Adelaide, reinforcing the smoke screen between her and the bar with another blast of noxious fumes, 'and any member of staff who din't come to the pub at all.'

'Not to mention,' added George glumly, 'anyone else in the vicinity. It could've been Farmer Sterne for all we know. Or one of his cows. All we've really done is rule out Quirk and Fotheringay. And you, I s'pose, Sister.' He thought about this for a moment. 'And we've only got your word for that.'

'To be precise, Georgie, you've only got my word

for any of it. If you don't believe me, then you've got nothing at all.' Sister Adelaide stubbed out her cigarette and inspected the packet on the table. It was empty. 'Right, then,' she said. 'That's yer lot. I'm out of ciggies so I'm off.' She downed the last of her stout and started to fold her *Racing Post*. 'But good luck to you, Georgie. I 'ope you can get Thanet off. 'E's not a bad lad really.'

Sister Adelaide stood and turned to face them. 'Bloomin' useless caretaker, obviously. But 'e's not a bad lad.' She touched her newspaper to her forehead in a parting salute and stepped through the fading bank of smoke towards the exit.

'Right,' said George, 'we'd better join the others in the back room, I s'pose.'

They listened for a moment to the noises coming from the back room. There was singing. And other sounds. All of it quite loud.

'It's quite a long ride,' said Daphne. 'Maybe we should head straight back.'

'Right you are,' said George, then gulped down his last swig of lemonade, and with a gentlemanly belch headed for the door.

TWENTY-ONE

George was tired. Tired, cold and miserable. He wanted to get back to St Rita's and climb into bed as soon as possible, but at the speed he was going that happy goal was still a long way off.

He was not the speediest cyclist at the best of times, and now, with heavy legs, tired and dispirited, his pedalling was laboured and slow.

'Can't you go any faster?' squawked Emily Lime, cycling alongside with no apparent effort.

'No,' he wheezed. 'I can't go any bloomin' faster. But you go ahead, Lime. Don't let us hold you—'

She was already out of earshot, zooming away, a diminishing spot of light on the road ahead.

'. . . back.'

'I wish we'd had some of those sandwiches,' said Daphne.

George's stomach nudged him with a hunger pang of agreement. 'Yuss. Although I didn't much fancy being stuck in that back room with Marion and the Fives. Sounded like it was starting to kick off as we left.'

George peered ahead of him. The light from Emily Lime's rear lamp had disappeared from view and the narrow lane that led from Pelham back to St Rita's was unlit. Furthermore, the thin sliver of moon had disappeared behind a cloud. George could only see the road for the few yards ahead of him that his cycle lamp revealed. Outside of that dim puddle of light was endless inky nothingness.

'Are you sure we're going the right way?' said Daphne.

'Oh yuss,' said George in a strained voice as he concentrated on keeping the edge of the verge within the beam of his lamp. 'I reckon we'll just about be able to see St Rita's once we get to the brow of this hill. There should still be some lights on in the teachers' rooms.'

He squinted into the dark ahead of them trying to make out how far off the brow of the hill might be. The truth was that he had no idea. He only knew they were going up a hill at all because his legs were complaining more than usual. Was this really the right way? They might easily have missed a turn in the dark.

George's cycle lamp flickered.

'Oh, no! Don't you dare!' he said.

The lamp went off entirely.

'Oh, heck!'

He gave it a thump, which made no difference except that it made him wobble across Daphne's path into the middle of the road.

Daphne veered past him. 'Stay close behind me,' she said. 'Follow my light.'

'Righto.' George pushed hard on his pedals and wobbled back to the side, grunting with the effort as he tried to keep up with the pulsing glow of Daphne's dynamo light, his one faint beacon in the darkness. And in that darkness, and the intense quiet of the night, George could hear everything there was to hear. The squeak of his bike wheels, a whine of breeze through unseen tree branches, the occasional rustling of some small creature in the hedgerows, the faint low buzz of . . . what *was* that?

Daphne called back something that George couldn't make out. But he could at least see the brow of the hill now as a dim light glowed behind it. The light grew brighter just as the faint low buzz grew louder. An engine, he thought. But not a car. The light and the noise grew and George could see the edges of the road now. He was too far out from the verge so he steered himself back over. He glanced up at Daphne as she started her way down the other side, saw her silhouette clear for a second against the bright oncoming light, then watched it disappear as she started her descent. He wondered at how loud the roar of the engine was now. A motorcycle, he thought. Going fast.

He heard something else then: a high, sharp animal noise maybe, almost lost in the sound of the engine. He looked for its source but saw nothing as the full beam of the oncoming headlight, too close, blinded him.

It was heading straight for him.

George cried out, wrenched his handlebars to the left and leaned hard into his pedals, steering away from the light. He felt the rush of wind as the motorbike raced past him, the bump of his front wheel hitting the verge then dropping suddenly. He felt himself falling, hung in the air, in space, in darkness, in absolutely nothing, as the roar of the motorcycle engine dropped in pitch and faded. He threw his hands out to brace himself for the impact when he hit the unseen ground. There was a brief rush of wind, a dull thud and—

TWENTY-TWO

George woke up.

This was a mistake.

Most of him was in pain, he felt confused, and he didn't know where he was.

He had been having a lovely dream about sandwiches and scones. Sleep had definitely been better, but there was no going back now. He wondered what time it was, whether it was day or night. He opened his eyes.

This was a mistake too.

It was definitely day. He knew this because there

was light, much more of it than was at all necessary. He squeezed his eyes shut again and, finding that this hurt too, groaned. While he braced himself for another go he heard footsteps on bare wooden floorboards.

Then when he opened his eyes again he found there was a blurry face mercifully blocking out the worst of the light.

'I say, Georgie, welcome back, old thing.' Marion's features sharpened into focus above him.

'Hello, Marion,' groaned George. 'Where am I?'

'Fourth form dorm, old thing. We found you unconscious at the roadside on the way back last night. Thought you'd be better sleeping it off here in Ronnie's old bed than in a ditch so I flagged down a passing motor, tipped the driver a couple of quid, and got you a lift back. What happened? Did you talk the landlord into selling you booze and you ended up too squiffy to cycle straight?'

'No . . .'

George pieced together some fragments of memory: darkness; a bright light; the loud whine of an engine.

'A motorbike ran us off the road!' he said.

'Well! That's a bit rum. Maybe *they* were drunk.'

'Oh no.' George shook his head, and quickly regretted it as he felt his brain rattle. 'It was deliberate. They came straight at . . . us.' He paused at that last word. Thought for a moment, his stomach churning. 'Daphne!' he said.

'Oh, she's all right,' said Marion. 'Took a tumble, same as you, but came round in the car. Bit shop-soiled but no bones broken. Think she made a better fist of landing than you, Georgie. You weren't thinking of a career as a paratrooper, were you? Only I'm not sure you're really made of the right stuff.'

George hauled himself up painfully onto his elbows and looked around. 'Where is she?'

'Where's who?' said Daphne, appearing at the door. 'I was just downstairs getting Nelly to fix our bikes up so we don't get trouble from the sixth formers.'

'Never mind the bloomin' bikes; are you all right?'

'More or less. At least, no bruises anyone is going to see. What about you?'

'Right as rain,' said George. 'So long as I don't move or speak.'

'Well, that sounds just about perfect.' Miss Bagley blew in like a warm gust. 'Keep you out of trouble for a bit, you daft clot. Thank you, Marion.' She gave a grateful nod as Marion galumphed happily out, then strode over wearing a casual grin. 'Reckon you'll pull through by the look of you,' she said, surveying George for damage. 'Think you can manage opening some post without any limbs falling off?' She waved a handful of envelopes in George's direction.

'And I think these are your photographs back from the chemist's, Miss Blakeway.' Miss Bagley handed a thicker envelope to Daphne, casting her an appraising glance as she did so. 'And no bones broken for you either?'

'No, miss. Thank you, miss.' Daphne gave a nod and began to tear open her package.

'Good. Well, I'll leave the telling-off for later, but for now just be aware that I take a dim view of my pupils gadding about outside of school grounds, at night, on stolen bicycles, and a dimmer view still if they fall off into a ditch. Don't do it again or I'll have your guts for garters.'

Miss Bagley gave them both a stern look while they each mumbled an apology, then she grinned.

'Just as well you hadn't been to the pub, or else I would've been *really* cross. Now, how come you're getting all the interesting post in the library these days? All I ever get is bills and complaints.'

George gave her a puzzled look. 'Nothing interesting here.' He held up a limp handful of papers.

'No? But there was a big parcel for Emily Lime that I dropped off to her on my way up. And you had those two packages in the last few days: the one I sent over with Erica a while back, and the one I gave you, you puddin'.' She gave George a prod.

His face moved about a bit as he thought back. 'Oh yuss. I had it on the tray to open after breakfast, but then . . . oh, we got distracted by cows. It must still be in the library somewhere. We never had one from Erica though.'

'No,' said Daphne. 'But she had one with her. I think she must have—'

'Liked the look of it and kept it for herself?' Miss Bagley gave a sorry nod. 'I think you may be right. Poor choice on my part to trust her in the first place really, but she happened to be passing. I shall have a word. Several, in fact, and well chosen. Now she's recovered from that bug I can really give her a piece of my mind.' Miss Bagley made for the door with grim intent. 'And no more nonsense from you pair either or you'll get the same.'

She stomped out.

George gave Daphne a grin. 'I wouldn't want to be in Erica's shoes, eh?' he said.

Daphne looked thoughtful. 'I think we'd better get to the library.'

George saw the seriousness in Daphne's face. He swung his legs out from the bed and heaved himself painfully into a sitting position.

'Why's that then?'

'I think . . .' Daphne edged towards the door. She turned to George, her face ashen. 'I think someone's trying to poison us!'

TWENTY-THREE

'Say that again,' gasped George as he stumbled after Daphne down the stairs.

'Don't you see? The first parcel arrived before the trip to the gallery, only we never got it because Erica stole it. Then the next day – the day of the gallery trip – she and her friends were too ill to go.'

'Yuss,' said George. 'Because they'd guzzled a whole box of chocolates the night before. Serves 'em right for not sharing.'

'But it wasn't even that big a box. Not enough chocolates to make three girls sick, at least. But it

271

was about the same size as the parcel Erica had that was really meant for us.'

'You mean . . . Erica stole our chocolates?' George was appalled. 'I'm appalled,' he said.

'If I'm right, though, they were poisoned, so it's lucky for us that she did. So we didn't get sick, and we did go on the gallery trip, and we started investigating . . .'

They reached the bottom of the staircase and turned for the library.

'And we got another parcel.' George's brain, engaged by the thought of chocolates, was kicking into gear now. 'And it was about the same size. I bet that was chocolates again. And poisoned again too. But we never even unwrapped them.'

Through a double door, round the corner, nearly there now.

'So when *they* didn't work . . .' Daphne broke into a trot.

'*Another* package.' George, for once, began to run without complaint.

'That Miss Bagley gave to Emily Lime ten minutes or more ago. Only it sounds like this one was bigger, so maybe whoever's trying to stop us has given up on poisoned chocolates now.'

'What do you mean?'

'I don't know.' Daphne was sprinting along the home straight now. 'How hard is it to . . . to make a bomb?'

'Oh, lumme!'

They dashed up the steps to the library door and burst inside.

'LIME!' yelled George. 'DON'T OPEN THAT—'

'I'm not sending it back,' said Emily Lime, scowling up at them from amidst a pile of shredded brown paper on one of the study tables and clutching a large hardback book to her chest. 'You can't make me.'

A terrific wave of relief passed through George. Then, straight after, an even bigger wave of anger.

'What...' he said, starting down the steps behind an outstretched arm and a very pointy finger, '... is *that*?'

'It's a book. Obviously.' Emily Lime hugged it tighter.

'And is it, by any chance, a stupidly expensive book that you have ordered from Stimpson's despite the fact that you know full well we haven't got any money left to pay for it?'

'No,' said Emily Lime. 'Of course not.'

George's pointy finger wavered, and his out-stretched arm fell to a less accusing angle. 'Oh,' he said.

'It's an understandably expensive book,' said Emily Lime, 'from an entirely different bookshop.'

'Lime!' George's hand balled into a fist.

'But it's a very good book.'

'I don't—'

'At least it has very good pictures. I can't read Dutch, so I don't know about the text. But we've got a Dutch dictionary in Languages, so...'

'You ordered a book *from Holland*?' spluttered

George. 'The postage alone will bankrupt us!'

'Probably,' said Emily Lime. She rummaged through the fragments of brown paper, picked one out and held it aloft. 'But look at the interesting stamps they used.'

It seemed from his expression that George did not care for the interesting Dutch stamps. To avoid the likely imminent explosion (and Hulky's reaction to it), Daphne placed a calming hand on George's shoulder.

'We should check that other parcel, George,' she said. 'Why don't you see if it's in the office?'

George stomped off, like a black cloud in noisy footwear.

'What is this extravagant book then, anyway?' said Daphne.

Emily Lime held it up for her to see.

'Abel van Koestell?' said Daphne. 'The painter who taught van Biergaarten?'

'Yes. I only ordered it because I thought it might help with your silly detective games. You'd think he might be at least a little grateful.'

They turned as George emerged from the office, holding aloft a brown paper parcel. He placed it on the table.

'*To the staff of St Rita's Library,*' Daphne read from the front. 'Typed address. Postmark says Pilkington.'

'Very ordinary stamps,' said Emily Lime.

George harrumphed and tore open the wrapping. 'Chocolates. You were right,' he said. 'And a card . . . *More chocolates for you all, in appreciation of all that you do* and it's signed *A well-wisher.*'

'You'd need a bigger box than that to properly appreciate a library,' said Emily Lime.

'You'd need for them not to be poisoned too,' said Daphne, plucking one of the chocolates out and turning it over. 'Look. See that mark there? I think that's where they injected it with something.'

George looked appalled. 'That's no way to treat a peppermint cream.' He took out two more of the chocolates and turned them over. Each had the same signs of tampering. 'And the fudge! And the raspberry parfait!'

Emily Lime and Daphne checked some more with the same result.

'It looks like they did all of them,' said Daphne.

'What kind of *monster* are we dealing with?' said

George. Then he contemplated the vanilla truffle he had most recently examined. 'Do you think if I had just *one . . .* ?'

'Put it back,' said Daphne, putting her hands in her pockets, but finding one hand obstructed by the envelope of photographs Miss Bagley had given her.

George placed the chocolate back in the box, with all the sad regret of someone waving goodbye to their sweetheart on a departing train.

'Yes,' he said. 'It's probably for the best. I suppose these are evidence now.' He thought for a moment. 'What should we do? Take them straight to the police?'

Daphne had taken the envelope from her pocket and torn it open. 'Mm?' she said absently.

'Or maybe we should get them analysed by Brady in the third form. She's pretty handy in a chemistry lab.'

Daphne, leafing through her photographs, did not reply.

'If we find out what's in them first,' George continued, 'we can get Woolley to call the police in. It'll sound better coming from her, I s'pose.'

When Daphne again failed to answer, George looked over at her. She was staring at one of the photographs, her lips silently twitching, as if she was concentrating hard on doing a tricky sum in her head.

'What do you think, Daffers?'

At last she looked up at him. 'Sorry?' She sounded distant.

'If we can prove the chocolates are poisoned, should we get Woolley to call the police in?' said George, with a generous dash of exasperation.

'No!' The firmness of Daphne's reply, and the stare that accompanied it, took George by surprise.

'Eh?' he said. 'Why not.'

Daphne held up the photograph. 'Because I think she sent them.'

TWENTY-FOUR

'Oh! I see!' said George, jabbing a finger at the photograph that Daphne had set down on the table. He frowned, tilted his head one way and then the other, then sent a hand rummaging through the dank jungle of his hair. 'Um, what do I see?'

Daphne sighed. 'You remember I was still taking photographs as we were leaving the gallery?'

'Yuss. Though it looks like you mostly got pictures of all the smoke.'

'Yes. But look: this one I took as we were getting out. You can see Miss Woolley here urging a girl to

leave. See?' Daphne pointed out the blurry figures in one corner of the picture.

George squinted at them. 'Just about, yuss,' he said.

'Then this is just after.' Daphne placed another photo next to the first. 'The girl's coming our way, but Miss Woolley—'

'Is heading back into the gallery.'

'Towards the Dutch room!'

'Maybe.' Emily Lime sounded doubtful. 'She could be going any number of different ways.'

'Where is she in the next photo?' said George.

'Well . . .' Daphne held up another photograph

with its back facing the others. 'I didn't take any more until we got outside. At least not deliberately. But—' She laid down the photograph on top of the others. 'While we were heading for the exit the shutter must have clicked by accident with the camera facing back the way we'd come. So it's mostly smoke and ceiling, and it's all skew-whiff...'

'Very modern,' said George. 'All those jaunty angles. Miss Deakins would approve, I'm sure.'

'But you can just see here, look...' Daphne tapped at a gap in the billowing clouds of smoke. 'There's the crime taking place!'

Framed by smoke, there was the painting being lifted down from its place on the wall by a pair of fuzzy hands.

'Heck!' said George. 'There's not much to go on, is there? It *might* be Woolley, I s'pose.' He shuffled the photos on the table. 'There's no other candidates in sight just before, at least as far as we can see. But then not much later she was unconscious and draped over the shoulder of a fireman carrying her out.'

'She seemed to be unconscious, at least, but that could have been a pretence.'

'Either way,' said Emily Lime, 'she didn't have a painting with her.'

'No. But perhaps she could have hidden it somewhere and then picked it up the following day. Remember she went back to smooth things over with the gallery director, Mr Montague?'

'Oh, yuss.' George remodelled an unruly mass of hair from one lumpy shape to another as he considered this. 'Sounds risky, though. Especially to steal a painting, just to leave it in Thanet's cottage and call the police. I know he's not much cop as a caretaker, but she's only been in the school five minutes. He can't already have annoyed her enough to want him locked up, surely.'

Emily Lime gave a snort that suggested that five minutes was ample as far as she was concerned.

'Unless . . .' Daphne took a breath. 'Do you remember what Molly Fox was saying?'

'Before Hulky knocked her into orbit?'

'Yes. She said, *What have you done with it?* What if she meant the painting?'

'Have you gone soft in the head, Daffers? The painting's back in the gallery. You've seen it there. Molly Fox has seen it there. You've seen Molly Fox seeing it there!'

'But I've been thinking: the way she was looking at it . . . it was as if she thought there was something wrong with it. As if, maybe, it was—'

'A forgery?' said Emily Lime.

George's face showed the painful evidence of deep thought for a short while. 'So you're saying Woolley stole the real *Canary*, planted a fake in Thanet's cottage, then tipped off the police?'

'Yes! That way she's got the genuine painting, the museum think they have it back, and the police are happy that they've caught their thief.'

'So she's stolen the painting but no one knows? I s'pose that makes sense.'

Daphne looked thrilled.

'Though I don't see why she'd go to all that trouble for a painting that's barely worth tuppence ha'penny.'

Daphne looked much less thrilled.

'Just the same, if there's even a chance you're right, then we only need to find the genuine *Canary* and we can prove Thanet innocent. We need to search Woolley's room.'

'Oh,' said Daphne, looking the very opposite of

thrilled. 'But how will we get in?'

George rearranged his face and hair as he considered this. 'I'll sort it,' he said. 'Meet me at the foot of the stairs in ten minutes.'

Emily Lime, of course, stayed right where she was with her book while Daphne made her way to her rendezvous with George. The bell went as she waited there and Daphne watched the teeming hordes of girls moving from one room to another until George arrived.

'Funny how everyone still moves about at the bell, isn't it?' mused George. 'Nobody's taking any notice of the teachers once they get there, mind, but mostly they're still going to where they're meant to be, even after Woolley made lessons optional.'

Daphne hadn't really thought about it. They started up the stairs and she noticed that although there was no shortage of bad behaviour going on around them, it was more muted than usual, as if the girls' hearts weren't in it.

'I suppose it's a bit odd for them,' she said. 'They're so used to not doing as they're told, but now they're not being told to do anything. With nothing to rebel against they're a little lost.'

'And *The Roar* is more lost than any of them,' said George, pointing out ex-head girl Cynthia Rawlinson amidst the throng, head and shoulders slumped. She looked as if she might at any moment sink entirely beneath the surface of the stream of girls flowing around her.

'I almost feel sorry for her.' George glanced after her as she made no attempt to resist the current and was swept away. 'Almost.'

They started up the second flight of stairs, towards the dorms and the teachers' quarters. Daphne looked nervous.

'Don't worry, Daffers,' said George. 'I know the timetable for everyone like the back of my hand and all of the staff are teaching now. Or at least they're all in classrooms downstairs. I don't suppose there's much learning going on anywhere.'

'And Miss Woolley? She doesn't teach.'

'Oh, she'll be in her office,' said George confidently as they reached the second-floor landing. 'Probably,' he went on, in a less certain mumble.

George's room was in among the staff bedrooms, and Daphne noticed its ominous whiff as they passed. A little further on George stopped at a door, pressed his ear to it for a moment, nodded to himself, then pulled a key from his pocket. He unlocked the door and pushed it open.

'You have a key?' said Daphne.

'Mmm . . . Miss Bagley has a full set of spares in her office. In case of emergencies. I went to see her and borrowed this 'un when she wasn't looking.'

He wafted Daphne in and followed close behind closing the door behind them. Morning light angled in through the net curtains dappling the rather carelessly made bed, a small pile of newspapers on the floor, a wooden chair and—

'There's an easel,' said George, pointing at the large, wooden, impossible-to-miss artist's easel dominating the centre of the room.

'Yes!' Daphne took a close look. 'No work in progress on it at the moment, but it's been used recently.' She dabbed a fingertip at a splodge of paint on the wood. 'Still wet.' She held up the newly coloured digit for George's inspection. 'And you can smell . . .'

George sniffed the air ruminatively. 'Oh yuss. That's the same smell as in the art room.' He shivered.

'What's wrong?'

'Dunno. I just don't like it. Makes me think of my last school, and . . . *cricket*, somehow.' He shuddered again. 'Horrible.'

'Why on earth . . .' Daphne shook her head. 'Oh, wait. What's that stuff that cricketers put on their bats? Some sort of varnish, I think . . .'

'Yes!' George's face lit up. 'Linseed oil! Of course! So that means . . .'

'What?'

'I dunno. That Miss Woolley is a secret cricketer?

I'm not sure that helps us.'

'Oh, wait. I think linseed oil is used with oil paints too!'

'Blimey!'

'Could Miss Woolley really have made a copy of the stolen painting, do you think?' Daphne said. 'I didn't know she could paint at all.'

George shuffled round the room taking in the rest of its contents. 'Well, I s'pose if you're planning a forgery then you don't go advertising the fact beforehand.' He thought about this for a moment as he looked under Miss Woolley's bed. 'Unless you're Lydia Whitford in the third form. She put a small ad in the *Chronicle* last term. And the last anyone heard she was on the run in Switzerland.'

'In any case,' Daphne said, 'Miss Woolley's been painting something, and whatever it is isn't here. But then, if we're right and the painting in the gallery is a fake, then what we're looking for is the genuine *Fish Seller's Canary*, and there's no sign of that either.'

George looked at the wardrobe and chest of drawers standing against one wall, and fluttered a hand in their direction. 'Um, you should probably . . .'

he said, blushing.

Daphne raised an eyebrow.

'There'll be, y'know . . . *lady garments* in there.'

'Oh, for heaven's sake!' Daphne opened in turn

each of the drawers and the wardrobe and searched
thoroughly within, taking care to leave no trace of
her intrusion. 'Nothing. She's got rid of it already. Or

perhaps she never even brought it back here,' she said.

'No, I think she must have. If she wanted to make a good enough fake to fool the gallery then she'd need the real one here to work from. Stands to reason. So presumably she had it here at least until I found the copy at Thanet's.' George considered the possibilities for a moment, his face contorting with the effort. 'She could still have shifted it since, but flogging stolen paintings is tricky at the best of times according to Sister Adelaide. Plus the whole thing was in the papers, which wouldn't help . . . So it's not likely she could sort a buyer quickly. I reckon she's still got it, for now.' His face relaxed as the last bit of thinking came to an end. 'And if it isn't here, most likely it's in her office.'

'Oh,' said Daphne, without any obvious enthusiasm. 'Good. So I suppose that means we'll—'

George was already out the door. 'Library first, then Woolley's office,' he called back to her.

'Oh, joy,' muttered Daphne and loped after him.

Emily Lime looked up from the expensive Dutch book as George burst into the library. Daphne followed him in with a polite lack of enthusiasm.

'Ah!' said Emily Lime. 'You're back. Good.'

Daphne, already some paces behind George, nearly fell over at the shocking news that Emily Lime was pleased to see them. This had never happened before.

Emily Lime flipped back a few pages. 'This book is really very good. Worth every guilder we paid . . . that is, every guilder we are *going* to pay for it. Although it being in Dutch is *very* irritating. It's slowing me down a lot. Why can't everyone just use English? It would make things so much simpler. I haven't even read half of it yet but Abel van Koestell is fascinating. It seems he was one of the most highly regarded painters in the country in his day, but when he died in a fire at his studio a lot of his work was destroyed so his reputation rests on the few paintings that still survive, which are—'

'Never mind your bloomin' book and your dead painter,' said George, looming messily over her. 'Woolley's the thief.'

'Surely you could have left the book behind for five minutes,' said Daphne as they marched down the corridor towards Miss Woolley's office.

'But I haven't finished it,' said Emily Lime, struggling to turn the pages of the Dutch dictionary with one hand and keep hold of the unwieldy art book in the other. 'It's very exciting.'

'Really?' Daphne wasted a withering look on her.

'Yes. Actually, it's virtually one of those mysteries you like so much. You see, van Koestell had a painting called—'

'We don't care, Lime,' said George. 'We're really quite busy with a mystery from *now* that matters a lot more because if we don't solve it then Mr Thanet will end up in prison for years. So you'll have to forgive us if we don't care *quite* so much about your bloomin' mystery of a Dutch fella who's been dead for two hundred and odd years. Now can—'

'Woolley!' said Daphne.

George looked where she was pointing. Emily Lime glanced over too as she turned a page. There, emerging furtively from her office, was the head. She stood outside the doorway for a moment, seemingly talking to herself. Then she gave a nod and closed the door, rather awkwardly, as she had a shopping bag in one hand and in the other a small painting.

'She's got the *Canary*!' said George. 'Come on!'

They set off towards the head. Woolley, in turn, went less steadily in the opposite direction.

'Excuse me, miss,' George called out. 'Could we just have a word?'

Miss Woolley, flinched, hesitated, then continued on away from them at a slightly faster shuffle.

'I'm sorry, children, I'm in rather a hurry. I'm, er—' She sped twitchily on, taking care to keep the painting turned away from them, but the children were gaining on her.

'Why don't we help you, then, miss?' said George. 'We're heading the same way. We can carry your things for you.'

He tried to grab at the painting but Miss Woolley pulled it away.

'That's ... very kind but, really, there's no need.'

George moved ahead of her now and Daphne came up alongside her, while Emily Lime trailed in her wake so that between them they had her boxed in.

'Really, children, wouldn't you be better off in a lesson?' Her head jerked round as she tried to keep track of all three of them, and she kept the painting facing the wall and close to it. 'Of course, you're free to do as you please,' she continued in a strained voice. 'But I really would prefer it if you gave me a little more space.'

'Oh, I'm sorry, miss,' said George. 'But we saw you had a painting, and we've been so inspired since the gallery trip that we just can't get enough of art. Give us a look, will you?'

'Actually,' said Miss Woolley, coming to a stop,

'I'd really rather not. It's . . . it's one I painted myself but it, um . . . didn't turn out very well. So I'm afraid I'm just too embarrassed to show it to you. Now, please . . .' Her voice began to crack. It sounded at once both tearful and angry. 'Just leave me alone, will you?'

'Oh, of course, miss,' said George, staying put.

'I didn't even want to do it,' said Miss Woolley, almost to herself now. 'Only Dr Gordon said that a hobby would help my nerves.' Her eye twitched alarmingly. '*Try painting*, he said. *It will relax you*, he said. As if anyone could relax trying to run this madhouse!' She stared at George and Daphne in turn, her eyes fixed. 'Do I look relaxed?' she said. And she did not. 'Does this . . .' She hesitated, then turned the painting to show them, held it right in front of their faces one after the other. 'Does *this* look relaxed?'

What Miss Woolley's painting lacked in technique it more than made up for in energy and primitive expression. It used a limited colour scheme of mostly black and violent red applied with great force. It was really quite frightening.

'It's very . . . modern,' said Daphne.

'It was meant,' seethed Miss Woolley, 'to be a

lovely vase of flowers! But once I started . . . Then after a while I was just stabbing and stabbing and stabbing at the canvas with my brush.' She was sobbing now. 'And—' Now her breathing faltered, air rasped in and out of her and her expression changed again, back from distress to fury. 'And I AM NOT RELAXED!' She threw the canvas to the floor, then stamped on it. Then with a scream of, 'No more art!' she launched the shopping bag back down the corridor, spilling paintbrushes and tubes of oil paint across the floor outside her office door. 'Not relaxed at all,' she said, then sank to the floor, weeping uncontrollably.

'Could you try to do that a bit more quietly?' said Emily Lime. 'I'm trying to read.'

'There, there,' said Daphne.

'Yes. There, there,' said George, sneaking a look at the soles of Miss Woolley's shoes, then giving Daphne a small shake of the head. 'Come on, miss. You need a bit of a rest. How about a nice sit-down and a cup of tea in your office?'

Miss Woolley shook her head. 'No. Don't want to go in my office.'

'Or we could see if we could find Miss Bagley?' said Daphne.

'No!'

'Well,' said Daphne, smiling gently, 'you can't just sit here in the corridor all day, can you?'

'I don't see why not,' said Emily Lime. 'She is the head, after all. She can do what she likes. Make lessons optional, unleash anarchy in the library . . .'

'Want to see Nursey,' said Miss Woolley.

'Nursey?' Daphne gave her a quizzical look. 'Do you mean . . . Matron?'

'At Wolfridge, Nursey was lovely. So kind. Take

297

me to Nursey.'

Daphne and George exchanged glances.

'Well, if that's what she wants . . .' said George.

They took her to the sanatorium and left her in the less than tender care of Matron, who was neither kind nor lovely.

'Good luck, miss,' said Daphne, as they made to leave.

'Oh, don't you worry,' said Matron. 'I'll take good care of her.'

George winced. 'That's what I'm afraid of,' he muttered.

'Now what?' said Daphne.

'For starters we should go and clear up all those paints in the corridor before the bell goes and they get trampled,' said George, setting off back towards Miss Woolley's office.

'Since when were you so concerned about tidiness?' Daphne eyed him suspiciously – the sight of him was evidence enough that cleanliness was not a major motivating force in his life.

'Well, no, you're right. But if we sell all that art gubbins that Woolley chucked away then we can maybe get close to being able to pay for Lime's bloomin' ridiculous Dutch book.'

'Not ridiculous,' said Emily Lime, with her nose still in it.

'Oh!' said Daphne as they turned the corner.

'Oh?' said George, then saw what Daphne had already seen. 'Oh! Oh bloomin' heck!'

The corridor was a mess. Many of the paint tubes had been trodden on and burst open and a trail of colourful footprints led away down the hallway.

'So much for that plan,' said George.

'Yes,' said Daphne. 'But look.'

George looked. Every other footprint had a clear crack across the sole.

'Oh!' he said.

'Well, quite,' said Daphne. 'Come on!'

The trail of footprints led to the art room. Daphne pushed open the door.

The wooden easels that had occupied the centre of the room the last time that George and Daphne had visited now lined two of the walls. With the centre empty, they had a clear view through to the back of the room where Miss Deakins, standing on a chair, was reaching for her abstract painting on the far wall. A shiver of realization made Daphne gasp.

'George,' she whispered, 'would you say that painting was about eleven and seven-eighths inches by eight and a quarter?'

Miss Deakins, still unaware that she was not alone, carefully took down the painting.

'I s'pose,' he whispered back. 'Why do . . . Oh!'

That last 'Oh!' was no longer a whisper, and Miss Deakins, hearing it, turned on her chair to see who had said it.

'Oh,' she said. 'Hello, children, can I help you?'

'Hullo, miss,' said George. 'Gone off that one, have you?'

Miss Deakins plastered a weak smile over her previous startled expression. 'Not at all. But, um, one has to keep changing things around.' She stepped down from the chair. 'Constant visual stimulation, that's the key.'

'Can we have it then?' said Daphne. 'For the library.' She followed George ambling across the floor towards the far wall. Emily Lime shuffled in behind her, still reading.

'Oh,' said George. 'Yes, good idea. Brighten the place up a bit.'

Emily Lime gave a disapproving grunt and turned a page.

Surprise froze on Miss Deakins' face. She shook it free. 'Well, I rather thought I might move it to my own room. Do you mind? Silly, I know, but I'm rather proud of it.'

'Oh!' said Daphne, her face suddenly illuminating. 'Yes! You must have a space for a picture, mustn't you?'

'Um . . .' said Miss Deakins. 'Yes. But I don't—'

'Since the one you got Mr Thanet to hang for you presumably isn't there any more. A picture you'd put into the frame from *The Fish Seller's Canary* so he'd get his fingerprints all over it!'

For a second, Miss Deakins frowned, but then her face flooded with sympathy. 'Oh, my dears. Now I know you're upset about dear Mr Thanet, but really, I—'

'Really,' said George, 'you need some new shoes.' He waved a hand at the trail of tell-tale paint footprints.

'Er . . .' said Miss Deakins.

'The jig is up, miss,' said George.

Miss Deakins opened her mouth as if to protest, but she said nothing. Then after a second or two she closed it again and gave a tiny nod. She took a slow, submissive step towards them, her shoulders slumped.

'Aha!' said Emily Lime, and slammed her book shut.

In the moment that Daphne and George were distracted by Emily Lime's sudden outburst, Miss Deakins launched herself between them. She barged into George, knocking him into Daphne, and sending them both sprawling to the floor. Then she pushed Emily Lime aside with an outstretched hand and sprinted for the door.

'Lime!' said George, picking himself up from the floor. 'What did you do that for?'

'What?' grumped Emily Lime.

'*Aha!*' said Daphne, wincing as she stood, then glaring at her.

'I got to a good bit in my book,' said Emily Lime. 'It was—'

'Unbelievable!' George seethed.

'On the contrary,' said Emily Lime as she picked her books up off the floor. 'It was entirely convincing. Now come on, or she'll get away.'

She set off sprinting after Miss Deakins, Daphne following in her wake.

'Oh, joy,' said George, bracing himself. 'Running. Why does there always have to be running?'

Miss Deakins exited the door that led to the playing fields well ahead of the children. Emily Lime stuffed her books under one arm to free up a hand to turn the door handle. Daphne and George caught up to her as she got it open.

'Leave the bloomin' books!' said George.

'No!' said Emily Lime. 'I haven't read the Acknowledgements yet.'

Then they were out the door and gazing across the fields.

'Where's she gone?' said Daphne as they scanned

frantically for any sign of Miss Deakins.

'Maybe,' said George, 'she's gone round to the bike shed to—'

A distant muffled yell interrupted him. 'Hey!'

Then the thrum of an engine, getting louder and more distinct until the unsteady figure of Miss Deakins on Miss Cosgrove's motorbike emerged from the side of the school and bumped and weaved onto the hockey field, her overcoat flapping behind her like a cloak, mud spraying up from the back wheel as it struggled to gain purchase on the slippery surface.

The children set off at a run towards her, up the slight slope at the side of the field. Miss Cosgrove, spanner in hand, flustered and furious, arrived by their side.

'I'll bloody kill her!' she said.

'We'll have to catch her first,' said George. 'And we don't have motorbikes.'

'No,' said Daphne. 'But we have to try.'

Miss Cosgrove and Emily Lime had already set off. George blew out an extravagant sigh and followed behind Daphne.

At first it seemed there was hope. Miss Deakins

had proved herself unsteady enough on a motorbike on a road. On muddy ground, and with a painting clamped under one arm, her progress was chaotic. The bike leaned from side to side, jagging from one direction to another, with the same seemingly random uncertainty as a bluebottle in flight. Then as the tyres lost their grip on the mud, Deakins lost her balance. She planted a foot to steady herself, which sent the bike pivoting round in a tight circle. By the time she wrenched her foot free, she was facing back the way she had come. The bike lurched and leaped and flew towards her pursuers. She yanked the handlebars round and swerved past Emily Lime, Daphne and Miss Cosgrove, but now she was heading straight for George.

For a split second George saw his own panicked expression mirrored in Miss Deakins' face, then he launched himself sideways out of the way. He felt Deakins' overcoat flapping against his leg as she sped past then landed, winded but unharmed, in the mud.

Miss Deakins wrestled the motorbike onto a new course and arced round, slaloming back between George and the others with a neatness and precision that would have been impressive if only she had intended it. Then she was off again, towards the woods, gaining speed, the rasping song of the bike's engine rising and falling as she worked her way up through the gears.

George peeled himself off the ground. Miss Deakins had reached the firmer ground of the lacrosse pitch now, and with the bike under better control she was pulling further and further ahead of her sprinting pursuers. George climbed to his feet and started after them anyway. And, fuelled by adrenaline, he was at least gaining on the others. But they were no match for a Triumph Thunderbird 6T motorcycle, however badly it was ridden.

Then Emily Lime's foot shot back from under her, kicking something round into the air behind her, and throwing her to the ground directly in Miss Cosgrove's path. Miss Cosgrove gave a sharp cry as she came down like a felled tree. Daphne slowed for a moment to adjust her course, then she too gave a yell and crumpled to the floor as whatever it was that had tripped Emily Lime ricocheted off her head and on towards George's face. He threw up his hands in self-defence and neatly caught what turned out to be a hockey ball. He ran on, past Daphne, then Emily Lime and Miss Cosgrove, casting each of them a concerned glance in turn, then set his sights back on the distant motorcycle and its rider, an unfamiliar fire inside him driving him on.

Miss Deakins was close to the edge of the woods now, but the trees before her were too dense to pick a path through. She looked round, saw George still distant, the others rising dazed from the ground, then turned the bike and rode along the edge of the wood, scanning it for the best route through. George stared into the shadows between the trees too, trying to work out where Deakins would choose. The clearest gap was right near—

Then maybe there was hope after all!

George ran on, his breath hoarse, trying to ignore his protesting lungs and his aching muscles. Deakins' route brought her closer to him as she rode past the gap, looped round and lined up the bike to enter the woods. George passed the hockey ball from his left hand to his right. Deakins came to a halt in front of the gap that he had hoped she would choose, stared into the woods, glanced back at George, revved the engine, tensed herself.

George gripped the hockey ball tight. He was still too far away. He pushed himself on, his heart pounding, dimly aware that he could hear the others behind him now.

Miss Deakins let out the clutch, the bike lurched forward . . . and stalled!

George ran on, his lungs burning, knuckles white around the hockey ball.

Deakins shot him a worried look. She kicked at the starter, once, twice . . .

George could see her panic now. There was just a chance. He dragged up an unhappy memory from his last school and conjured the voice of his old games teacher.

Deakins kicked again and the bike's engine roared to life.

Come on, boy! Left arm forward, right arm back.

Deakins let out the clutch.

Left foot down . . .

George pushed off hard from his right foot, planted his left firmly onto the grass, sighted along his outstretched left arm.

The bike crept forward.

Step through . . .

George's body pivoted and twisted. He threw his weight forward.

The bike eased towards the gap in the trees.

And throw!

George's arm windmilled round, with all his weight behind it, every muscle and sinew at its limit, hurling the ball . . .

. . . which arced high over Miss Deakins' head and disappeared into the woods.

Useless boy!

All effort spent, George's legs buckled beneath him and he fell, staring desperately into the shadows between the trees as the bike sped into them.

Then he called one rasping word out into that darkness.

'FETCH!'

A large shape detached itself from the rest of the shadows and, mooing excitedly, sprang towards where the ball had landed, directly into the path of the motorbike. Miss Deakins yanked at the handlebars and veered sharply left. The front wheel struck a root, bounced up, came back down aiming straight for a tree. Deakins wrenched the handlebars round again, steering for the gap between tree and cow, regained control and gunned the engine once more. The bike leaped forward towards an easy path through the woods.

'Moo!' said the cow again as the rope she was tied with pulled tight behind her, catching Deakins across the chest and yanking her from her saddle. The bike sped on without her. Deakins fell with a sharp cry, landed hard on her back, and lay still. There was a dull thump as the motorcycle came to an unseen stop somewhere among the trees. The cow gave another brief moo and then started to chew at the undergrowth.

'Good girl, Myrtle,' wheezed George, still on his hands and knees.

Daphne passed him at a trot.

'Quick,' said George, 'before she runs off.'

'I don't think she's getting up,' said Daphne.

Miss Deakins lay absolutely still.

'Oh God!' Miss Cosgrove sprinted ahead of Daphne, urgency close to panic in her cracked voice. 'Is she OK?' In a few swift long strides she was by Miss Deakins' side. 'Oh God! Oh God! Oh God!' And past her into the woods.

Daphne arrived beside Miss Deakins' side a moment later. She knelt down and pressed her finger to one of the art mistress's wrists.

'Is she all right?' said Emily Lime, glancing over at Daphne with no trace of concern in her voice.

'Not as bad as I'd feared,' said Miss Cosgrove, wheeling her motorbike back through the trees. 'Bit of a dent in the mudguard and a couple of broken spokes, but— Oh. You meant *her.*'

Daphne threw Miss Cosgrove a disapproving frown.

'Yes,' said Daphne. 'At least she's still alive, I think. I don't actually know where you find a pulse, but her chest's moving so she's definitely breathing.'

'Lucky her,' gasped George, arriving at last. He bent over, hands on knee. 'Now where's that bloomin' painting?'

Daphne looked round then rose, took three steps and pulled the canvas from a bush.

'It was lucky to have a soft landing,' she said. 'The only damage is to the top layer of paint.' She held up the canvas in one hand and pointed to a crack in the paint with the other. 'You see? And it looks like, underneath . . .' She pulled at the crack and dislodged a fragment of paint, causing a new crack to snake across from the first. She pulled away more chips of paint, working outwards to reveal a glowing yellow patch of another image beneath.

'The *Canary*!' said George.

'Not only that,' said Emily Lime. 'But—'

'Hang on,' said Miss Cosgrove, propping her bike on its kickstand. 'That's the painting that was stolen, isn't it? But if that's here then what have they got in the gallery now?'

'That,' said Daphne, 'is a long story.'

'Longer than you think,' said Emily Lime, pointing at her book. 'And more complicated. I've just read the Acknowledgements in this excellent book and—'

'The *Acknowledgements*?' George, still red-faced but breathing more or less normally now, joined them. 'Whoever reads the Acknowledgements? And in a Dutch book, while running after a motorbike chasing an art thief?'

'I do,' said Emily Lime. 'Obviously. And it's a good job I did or we wouldn't know about Miss Deakins' accomplice.'

'What?' said Daphne. 'You mean she was working with someone else?'

Emily Lime gave her a pitying glance. 'That *is* what accomplice means. And how else would she manage to get the painting down from the gallery wall quickly enough not to be seen? How else could she hide it in the gallery and later retrieve it without it being detected? *And*, most importantly, how else would she know how valuable it is?'

'You've changed your tune,' said George. 'I thought you said it was next to worthless.'

'Oh, it is,' said a voice from the shadows.

They all looked up as a figure emerged from the darkness of the woods.

'So you certainly wouldn't want to risk your life for it.'

He stepped into the light, raised a shotgun to his shoulder and aimed it straight at Daphne.

TWENTY-SIX

'**M**r Montague?' George stared at the director of the Pilkington Art Gallery with all the contempt he could muster. 'So it was an inside job. Gah! Men in suits and arty crafty types: you just can't trust any of them.'

'Quite correct,' said Montague, swinging the shotgun round in George's direction. 'Especially not when they're armed. So you just stay right where you are, I'll take the painting from your friend here, and no one need get hurt.' He edged sideways towards Daphne, who offered up the painting in a trembling hand.

'Actually,' said Emily Lime. 'It's *Professor* Montague, isn't it?'

Surprise flitted across Montague's face.

'Professor Montague is thanked in the Acknowledgements of this book.' Emily Lime lifted the van Koestell book. 'He's an expert on Dutch art, and Abel van Koestell in particular.'

Montague was beside Daphne now. He swung the gun barrel round in her direction as he took the painting from her trembling hand.

'He knows that a lot of van Koestell's work was lost in a fire. But he also knows that just before that fire Jakob van Biergaarten had been thrown out of van Koestell's studio.'

Montague took a step backwards, then another, then swung the shotgun round in Emily Lime's direction.

'One of the paintings that was supposedly lost in the fire was called *The Harbour Master's Cat*. Van Koestell's records show that it was 300 millimetres by 210. George, you're good with numbers, what's that in inches?'

'Um, let me see, that's just under twelve inches

by, er, about eight and a quarter. But I don't—'

'Oh,' said Daphne. 'Eleven and seven-eighths inches by eight and a quarter! The same as *The Fish Seller's Canary*!' She turned to face the retreating Mr Montague. 'You think van Biergaarten stole *The Harbour Master's Cat*, then painted over it!'

'So underneath the worthless painting,' said George, 'is one by this van Wotsit fella that's worth an absolute packet?'

'Yes,' said Emily Lime.

'And with the fake *Canary* on show at the gallery' – Daphne gave Montague a cold stare – 'and Mr Thanet convicted of the theft, you and Deakins would get away scot-free.'

'Not very likely now though, is it?' said George.

Montague stopped backing away and seemed to consider this. Even in the cold winter air there was a sheen of sweat on his face now. With the painting in his left hand he was holding the shotgun none too steadily one-handed in his right.

'You think you're so clever, don't you?' he snarled.

'Yes, of course,' said Emily Lime, shuffling sideways to move away from the others. 'I read.'

Montague's face boiled with rage. 'I ought to–'

His face twitched. He turned towards Emily Lime, raised the shotgun. His mouth tightened into a furious crooked line.

'Don't—' cried Daphne.

Montague's face screwed itself into a sneer. 'Don't tell me—'

A faint rustling came from the undergrowth behind him, then a dull grunt.

Something blurred through the air to meet the back of Montague's head with a loud crack. Montague looked oddly shocked, his eyes wide and his mouth hanging open. In the same instant, the shotgun bucked in his hand and both barrels erupted with a deafening roar.

Then, as startled crows took flight from the branches above, Professor Montague's head lolled to one side, his legs crumpled and he dropped face down to the ground.

Daphne and George snapped their heads round to look at Emily Lime who stood quite still, her empty hand held out to her side, and let out a howl of pain.

'Emily!' said George.

Emily Lime slowly raised her horror-filled eyes to his, her face pale.

'My book!' she cried. 'He shot my book!'

They all turned to look at the van Koestell book, lying on the ground several paces behind Emily Lime, a huge ragged hole blown out of its middle.

'For goodness' sake, Lime!' said George.

'Better that book than your head,' said Molly Fox, stepping out from behind a tree.

'Crikey!' said Daphne. 'Where did you spring from?'

'I was hiding out in Mr T's cottage. When I saw you all racing against a motorbike I came out to see what was going on. Then I spotted this one' – she pointed at Montague, face down and still – 'scuffling with Farmer Sterne in his field and knocking him out.'

'Crikey!' said Daphne. 'I wouldn't have thought Mr Montague would win that fight. He must be stronger than he looks.'

'Not really.' Molly Fox gave the unconscious Montague a disdainful look. 'Sterne slid over on a cowpat and hit his head on a fencepost that knocked him out cold. When he took Sterne's shotgun, I thought I'd best keep out of sight, but I followed him at a safe distance. Luckily, I found a hockey ball and managed to bean him with it before he pulled the trigger.'

'But he *did* pull the trigger!' shrieked Emily Lime. 'He murdered my book!'

'But not you, Emily Lime,' said Daphne, kneeling beside the unconscious Montague and lashing his hands behind his back with her tie. 'It was a good shot, Molly. Thank you.'

'Wasn't bad, was it?' Molly grinned. 'I was always quite handy at the coconut shy at the village fete too. Deakins and the museum fella were in on it together then, were they? Oh, maybe you should truss her up too. I think she's coming round.'

A warbled groan rose from the stricken art mistress. Miss Cosgrove stepped towards her. 'Leave that to me,' she said. 'Why don't you all go to Miss Woolley's office and telephone the police.' She gave Molly Fox a brief smile. 'This lot can explain it all to you on the way over.' She considered this for a moment and frowned. 'And then they can explain it to me when you get back.'

It took quite some time to explain everything to Inspector Bright when the police arrived. It was all quite complicated and George kept getting bits of it wrong, then Daphne would do her best to correct him, and the whole narrative was constantly interrupted by Emily Lime insisting that the destruction of library property was the most important charge to be answered, not these minor matters of theft, forgery or the assault of Farmer Sterne.

Further delays were provided by Constable Hawkins needing a lot of help with his spelling as he took notes, and occasional interjections from

Miss Deakins and Mr Montague who by the end had regained consciousness just enough to speak, but nowhere near enough to make any sense. But the inspector was eventually convinced that it was the semi-conscious art teacher and art gallery director who were the ones who needed to be arrested, and not the assistant and assistant assistant librarians, Deakins and Montague were first untied, then handcuffed, and then led away burbling incoherently to the waiting police cars.

'And you say this is a painting over a painting . . . over a painting?' said Inspector Bright, inspecting the rather sorry-looking cracked surface of the stolen canvas.

'Almost certainly,' said Emily Lime. 'Of course it will have to be X-rayed to be sure.'

'Naturally,' said the inspector. He waved the painting at a constable. 'Bung this in the boot of the car, will you, Charlie?'

'If we're right,' Emily Lime continued, 'then, once appropriately cleaned and restored, it will be worth several hundred thousands of pounds.'

Inspector Bright considered this. 'And maybe wrap it in a blanket for safety,' he said.

The constable gave a nod and carried the painting away.

Bright turned his attention to Emily Lime. 'Well done, Miss Lime,' he said. 'And thank you for your help in this matter.'

'Never mind that,' said Emily Lime. 'How much is the reward?'

Inspector Bright gave her a stern look. 'The Pilkington and District Constabulary does not offer cash incentives to encourage what should, in any case, be merely the civic duty of the citizens it has sworn to protect.'

Emily Lime's face screwed up in distaste.

'However,' the inspector went on, 'I shall be happy to inform the trustees of the Pilkington Gallery that they might wish to show you their appreciation with, perhaps, a small donation to library funds.'

Emily Lime considered this. 'Tell them we would prefer a very large one,' she said.

Inspector Bright's face wrinkled in amusement. 'I'll let them know,' he said. 'In the meantime, we'll need statements from all of you. Could you come back to the station with us for a chat?'

'And leave the library unattended?' said Emily Lime. 'I hardly—'

'I'm sure the sergeant could lay on some tea and biscuits. Possibly even cake.'

'Oh, I think the library could spare us for an hour or two,' said George. 'While we do our civic duty.'

Daphne grinned.

'That's very selfless of you,' she said.

Following Inspector Bright's lead, they set off across the playing fields.

'Oh!' said George. 'We can take some tea and biscuits in to Mr Thanet too, and give him the good news.'

'Make him promise to finally oil our door hinges

first,' said Emily Lime.

'Actually,' said Inspector Bright, 'we'll call ahead and have him released at once.' He turned to Miss Cosgrove. 'Perhaps you could take us to the head's office. We can use her telephone.'

'Yes, of—'

'Miss Woolley isn't in her office at the moment,' said Daphne. 'She's—'

'Over there,' said George, with surprise in his voice.

They all turned to see two distant figures moving quickly alongside the rear of the school.

'Is that Matron she's running away from?' said Miss Cosgrove.

'Yes,' said George. 'Maybe she's not so mad as I first thought, then.'

They watched as Matron and Miss Woolley, pulling long sunset shadows in their wake, ran towards the wall at the western boundary of the school grounds.

'Although it is a *bit* mad to go that way, I suppose. I mean, how does she think she'll—' They stopped for a moment to properly appreciate the scene playing out before them. 'Well, who'd've thought old

Woolley could be that good at climbing trees? She was over that wall in no time.'

'She's never coming back, is she?' said Daphne.

'I said she wouldn't last a week,' said George.

'Come *on*!' squawked Emily Lime. 'If we must leave the library then at least let's get it over with. The sooner we make our statements, the sooner we can get back. There's so much to do. I have important plans to make, you know.'

'Of course you do,' said George with a weary smile, as he and Daphne set off again.

'You know,' Daphne said, 'that however much the reward ends up being—'

'She's already planned how to spend *much* more than that,' said George. 'Yes, I do.' He sighed as he watched Matron trudging forlornly back towards the school. Then he smiled. 'But I'll worry about that later. For now, I'm concentrating on tea and biscuits.'

'And,' said Daphne, 'possibly even cake.'

Acknowledgements

Thanks are due for help in the making of this book to the following lovely people:

To Jeremy de Quidt for his superior knowledge of varieties of cow pat; to my old mate Tim Clarke, and Jonny Hewitt of Red House Farm, for cow advice; to Bridget Blankley for knowing about 1954 public telephones; to Ollie Crabb for knowing about pubs (who'd've thought it?); and to Si Williams for advising me about the evolution of the hockey ball.

To Anthony Hinton who edited with care, skill and (sadly very necessary) patience; to Ness Wood who designed the book inside and out with customary brilliance; to Sue Cook whose copy editing saved me from many embarrassing mistakes; and to David Fickling and all at DFB for watching over it all.

And to Pam, for the excellent chart. And for everything else.

EMILY LIME
LIBRARIAN
DETECTIVE

THE PENCIL CASE